Southern Fried Farce

Southern Fried Farce

A Buffet of Down-Home Humor from the Best of Southern Writers

Edited by Henry Oehmig

jefferson
press

January 2008

Copyright © 2008 by Henry Oehmig

All rights reserved.

ISBN: 978-0-9778086-8-7
Library of Congress Control Number: 2007938387

Book and jacket design by AuthorSupport.com
Editing by Henry Oehmig and Arlene Prunkl
First Printing January 2008
Printed in the United States of America

Published Jefferson Press

jefferson
press

808 Scenic Highway
Lookout Mountain, TN 37350

No part of this book may be reproduced or utilized in any form by any means, electronic or mechanical, including photocopying and recording, or by any information storage and retrieval system, without the prior written permission by the copyright owner unless such copying is expressly permitted by federal copyright law. Jefferson Press is not authorized to grant permission for further uses of copyrighted selections printed or reprinted in this book without the permission of their owners. Permission must be obtained from individual copyright owners as identified herein.

Copyright Acknowledgements

"Flagged, Flim-Flammed, and Fingerprinted" by Maria D. Baisier, penname M.L. Davis. Copyright © 2008 by Maria D. Baisier.

"Afternoon with a Buck" by Roy Blount Jr. First published in *Camel's Are Easy, Comedy's Hard*. Copyright © 1991 and 2008 by Roy Blount Jr. Permission granted by author.

"Man Showers, Faux Fireplaces, and a Doorbell that Chimes the Theme to *Rhinestone Cowboy*" by Lisa Daily. Copyright © 2008 by Lisa Daily.

"In Cold Mud" by Jim Dees. Copyright © 2008 by Jim Dees.

"I'm Not Leaving Until I Eat This Thing" by John T. Edge. First published in *The Oxford American*. Copyright © 2008 by John T. Edge. Reprinted by permission of the author.

"Down in Mexico with Vic, Big Vicious, and Bernadette" by Clyde Edgerton. Copyright © 2008 by Clyde Edgerton.

"Bit Part" by Tom Franklin. First published in *The Oxford American*. Copyright © 2008 by Tom Franklin. Reprinted by permission of the author.

Excerpt from *The Long Home* by William Gay. Copyright © 1999. Permission granted by MacAdam/Cage Publishing.

"Meat-Smoking Son of a Gun" by David Magee. First published in *The South Is Round*. Copyright © 2007 by David Magee. Permission granted by Jefferson Press.

"Judging the Sibling Summer Olympics" by Lisa Earle McLeod. Copyright © 2008 by Lisa Earle McLeod.

From *Boy with Loaded Gun*, by Lewis Nordan. Copyright © 2000 by Lewis Nordan. Reprinted by permission of Algonquin Books of Chapel Hill.

"Sex Devil," published in *The Mysterious Secret of the Valuable Treasure*, by Jack Pendarvis. Copyright © 2005. Permission granted by MacAdam/Cage Publishing.

"Meow...It's Happy Hour" by Susan Reinhardt. Copyright © 2008 by Susan Reinhardt.

"The Wrestler and the Fan" by Celia Rivenbark. Copyright © 2008 by Celia Rivenbark.

"The Delicate Lives of Amphibians" by George Singleton. Copyright © 2008 by George Singleton.

"The Little Fat Ballerina" by James Whorton Jr. Copyright © 2008 by James Whorton Jr.

"Sally the Screamer" by Ed Williams. Copyright © 2008 by Ed Williams.

Contents

Disclaimer: An Introduction. ix

JACK PENDARVIS 1
Sex Devil (fiction)

CLYDE EDGERTON 7
*Down in Mexico with Vic, Big Vicious,
and Bernadette (non-fiction)*

CELIA RIVENBARK 23
The Wrestler and the Fan (non-fiction)

GEORGE SINGLETON 33
The Delicate Lives of Amphibians (fiction)

SUSAN REINHARDT. 41
Meow...It's Happy Hour (non-fiction)

ROY BLOUNT JR. 51
Afternoon with a Buck (non-fiction)

LEWIS NORDAN 65
from <u>Boy with Loaded Gun</u> (non-fiction)

M.L. DAVIS 77
Flagged, Flim-Flammed, and Fingerprinted (non-fiction)

LISA EARLE MCLEOD 87
Judging the Sibling Summer Olympics (non-fiction)

CONTENTS (CONTINUED)

JAMES WHORTON JR. 95
The Little Fat Ballerina (fiction)

WILLIAM GAY 107
from The Long Home (fiction)

TOM FRANKLIN 117
Bit Part (non-fiction)

DAVID MAGEE. 127
Meat-Smoking Son of a Gun (non-fiction)

JOHN T. EDGE. 137
I'm Not Leaving Until I Eat This Thing (non-fiction)

LISA DAILY 143
Man Showers, Faux Fireplaces, and a Doorbell That Chimes the Theme from Rhinestone Cowboy (non-fiction)

JIM DEES 151
In Cold Mud (fiction)

ED WILLIAMS 161
Sally the Screamer (non-fiction)

Contributors. 175

DISCLAIMER: AN INRODUCTION

In this age of grudges and unprecedented access to people, it is necessary for the editor of an anthology to open with a short, fault-deflecting, litigation-ducking disclaimer. The reason? I have already divined there will be complaints. Complaints such as "This effing book of Southern humor isn't funny one bit—why weren't jokesters like Carrie Crabtree included, or that 'Balding' Ernest Spalding guy? You call this an anthology? It doesn't even make a half-decent doorstopper."

On other sleepless nights in the lead-up to this book, I imagined still more dismissals of *Southern Fried Farce*, a chorus of nasally voices condemning it as too silly, obnoxious, vulgar, or discordant to be taken seriously. Okay, fair enough. Anyone finding such faults may now dive back into their dusty, rare catalogs of entomology. And be sure to take any lingering austerity with you. The one thing I, with the contributors' help, have attempted to eradicate from these pages as if it were polio or the pine beetle is *Dry Seriousness.*

Back to the disclaimer. This is the South, after all—where everybody at least knows somebody who knows you. Combine that with Internet searches and good, ol' fashioned phone books, and there's no way for the respectable editor of an anthology to dodge the "feedback" of readers. So before you accidentally mail my uncle a discouraging letter, or mistakenly dial up my parents' house asking for the no-good anthologist they call son, let me first say this:

The following Work, titled Southern Fried Farce, *is not intended to be a comprehensive gathering of every Southern writer who wrote something funny. Furthermore, the editor of said anthology in no way guarantees the readers' unanimous satisfaction and will not be held accountable for any debts (psychiatric, medical, etc.) incurred by a reader following the perusal of these pages. In the non-event that you haven't laughed upon finishing this Work, you should have a family member check your pulse.*

No animals were harmed during the production of this Work.

There. Being relieved of liability, I would now like to propose that the advantages of reading this anthology far exceed the risks.

When I set out to assemble a book of Southern laughs, it was my goal to collect a variety of prose that would both entertain readers and expose the diversity of farce from or about the contemporary Southland—not to compile an exhaustive tome of the region's humor. As it happens, the latter challenge may prove impossible.

The text that comes closest to capturing this enduring but amorphous literary tradition is *Roy Blount's Book of Southern Humor*. In his Norton anthology, the master humorist, Blount, provides a wide assemblage of comical writings spanning from colonial days to the Clinton administration. So you might assume after such a process of research and discovery that Blount would have won some diamond-like understanding of Southern humor—clear, hard, multi-faceted, finite. Well, not exactly. In an article for *The Oxford American* called "Pursuing Southern Humor," Blount opines that "mounting an expedition into Southern humor—there is a lot of uncharted territory out there—and emerging with a tidy treasury of amusement would be like disappearing into the Amazon jungle and coming back toting a representative petting zoo."

Faced with a smaller pool of writers and their work—one narrowed by, oh, a few centuries—my job with this anthology was a bit easier. Still, the dilemma remained: how does one piece together a complete representation of Southern humor when the genre itself resists clear definition or, as Blount puts it, "is an irregular thing to collect"?

I do not pretend to know. But what I do know is this—the following stories and essays have been crafted by writers from or living in the South, and they are funny. Knee-slapping, button-busting funny. So while this anthology boasts no designs of finding and revealing all the extraordinary critters to have walked the dense forest of Southern comedy, it does manage to showcase some of its best current humorists—or if you prefer the jungle analogy, an impressive group of three-toed sloths, jaguars, and spider monkeys. (My apologies to the contributors.)

I also wondered early on how best to describe such a book. An anthology, yes, but the word does harbor an air of seriousness. One term that kept popping into my head— it must have been around lunchtime—was *buffet*, as in "A Buffet of Down-Home Humor from the Best of Southern Writers." It's odd, but adequate, I think. Admittedly, such a subtitle threatens to have at least one literalist reader sit down with this book, tear it apart, and begin digesting it. (Yet another reason to open with a disclaimer.) Regardless of this hazard, the idea of a buffet—something uniquely Southern in the deep-fried, all-you-can-eat tradition— seems to be a peculiar match. I would love to go on and on for pages trying to mine all the metaphors of buffet-style eating, but for now I'll spare you and limit myself to these two: #1. Have you ever considered how the different trays of green beans, country-fried steak, cornbread, collards greens, etc. mimic the familiar but disparate offerings of Southern humor? #2. A reader cannot fully appreciate this rich, assorted literary genre until the separate pieces are laid out side by side, allowing him or her to pair complementary items, in essence to top mashed potatoes with barbecue baked beans for an overwhelming experience of...

Oh forget it—this is just making me hungry and confused.

Seventeen writings appear between these covers; of them six count as fiction and the rest non-fiction. Each adds its own flavor and brand of Southern humor, and the result is a feast of hilarious tales, wondrous oddities, and dazzling wit capable of sating the appetite of any laugh-longing reader.

In the opening piece, you will find a query letter proposing a comic book series. This isn't based on any ordinary caped crusader, mind you, but a hero who could only spring from the mind of Jack Pendarvis. The protégé of a high school janitor trained in a "rare form of karate called Jah-Kwo-Ton," Sex Devil is forced to battle his nemesis, Black Friday, and at the same time becomes intimate with Black Friday's girlfriend. Wondering why Sex Devil is worthy of such a name? Let's just say it comes from his large endowment of...special powers.

Following this is Clyde Edgerton's first-hand account of catching a wild crocodile known as Bernadette on a gorgeous, deserted beach in Mexico. Read on as Clyde's fearless buddy, Vic, having recovered from two separate heart surgeries, fights through the crashing surf to ambush and dive on top of the sunbathing Bernadette. Meanwhile, Clyde watches from a safe distance at the top of the beach. I should point out that Clyde does manage to hold the captured croc by the end—a feat few people can claim.

Next comes Celia Rivenbark's latest essay, "The Wrestler and the Fan." This nostalgic piece will make anyone long for the good old days in the South when wrestling was more than just wrestling. Get ready to relive the spectacle, the grand choreography, and drama that once thrived in sweaty community armories throughout Dixie in the tradition of small-time, Southern-style wrestling. Forget today's pay-per-view and pyrotechnic shows—Rivenbark reminds us of the sport in its purest form, when doctors and little old ladies in the crowd could engage and verbally spar with the athletes.

Also venturing back to simpler times, George Singleton's "The Delicate Lives of Amphibians" is the coming-of-age story of young Stet Looper. Growing up in a "rock-laden, thrill-barren, unbalanced speck of unwritten laws"—it's a place in South Carolina—Stet is taught the value of a dollar and also not to squeal on his old man. It includes all the makings of a quintessential Southern humor story, complete with a subterranean hoochie-coochie show, a pedophile police deputy, and the further endangerment of an already endangered species.

The next two *true* tales push the boundaries of non-fiction and take further strides in explaining the Southerner's relationship with members of the animal kingdom. First, Susan Reinhardt introduces us to her family's alcoholic kitty, rescued from keg parties and fraternity house squalor. This lovable, boozy cat, though vicious on a dry spell, becomes the drinking buddy of Susan's reluctant father after her mother has found religion. They share a quiet, solid bond—her father and the cat—which ultimately leads to a decision and purchase that will last for eternity. And in a not-so-cuddly encounter, Roy Blount Jr. revisits the afternoon during which he narrowly escaped a gouging from a rut-crazed whitetail buck...in his neighbors' yard...while trying to retrieve a red-sequin skating dress out of his neighbors' house. You will just have to read it to believe it, and then it's still hard to believe.

Another perfectly ridiculous episode follows. This is the tale of the Amazing Technicolor Effing Machine, taken from the eponymous chapter of Lewis Nordan's memoir, *Boy with Loaded Gun*. Say you aren't familiar with such a device? Read and prepare to be surprised. Just a hint: it's lewd, it's absurd, it's an incredibly wild and hilarious lift to the pain and sobriety dominating the author's life at that time. And touching on this theme of finding the humor in hard times, New Orleans writer M.L. Davis pokes fun at the bureaucracy that plagues her home city in the wake of Hurricane Katrina. With patience and dignity, Davis, a teacher, adheres to her job's new requirement that she must be fingerprinted. But first she has to get a new driver's license. Then she is flagged for not having insurance on a car her son sold two years prior, and so begins her trouble. Lucky for us, she was not arrested in the process of becoming certified for work and was able to contribute this entertaining essay.

Lecturer and syndicated columnist Lisa Earle McLeod takes plenty of self-deprecating jabs as she dishes out the truth about her extended family's annual vacation. Not so much a relaxed group gathering as it is a heated sibling competition, McLeod explores the nuances of judging one's close and not-so-close family members. You may want to keep a notebook handy. Move over, Emily Post—this Southern lady knows etiquette *and* has a keen wit. She also keeps score.

Another Southern lady, albeit three years old, is the subject of James Whorton Jr.'s story, "The Little Fat Ballerina." Here, a dad escorts his young daughter to Miss Nadia's School of Dance in Kingsport, Tennessee, where he overhears the Russian head instructor commenting that his girl is too chubby to make a good ballerina. He reacts as any father would—with a mixture of tenderness and rage. He debates the incident with his wife and even brings it up with other mothers at the ballet school for their disapproval. By the end, all the tension and heated emotions are resolved, as they so often are, by a stop at the Dairy Queen for a dip-top.

Next we shift from Kingsport to the rural landscape surrounding Ackerman's Field, Tennessee, territory of William Gay's first novel, *The Long Home*. It's easy to get swept up and carried off by the lyricism of Gay's sentences and his startling descriptions of the natural world, but let nothing distract you from the wicked comedy of this passage concerning a hog manure thief. What begins as a mystery for farmer William Tell Oliver soon spirals into an impromptu biology lesson for a misguided, suspicious youth.

From 1940s, small-town Tennessee, we take a little bitty jump to present-day Hollywood. "Bit Part" is Tom Franklin's exposé on what really goes on at a Tinseltown Leading Man Party, where no true Southerner really belongs. While mingling at Kevin Costner's pool soirée, Franklin sticks out like a drunk in a choir, with his faded jeans, plain white shirt, and general goodwill. He watches with detached amusement as celebrities such as Garry Shandling and David Spade flirt with a crowd of puckish, half-nude models, and he dreams of a day when the tables are finally turned: when the dollar bills start rolling in, and Costner and all the lovely women of the world take notice.

The next two essays lead us back to familiar terrain, and more importantly, remind us of our carnivorous identity. In "Meat-Smoking Son of a Gun," David Magee describes recent trends in the most sacred possession of any Southern male: the hallowed smoker/grill. Would you believe they are now equipped with diesel engines? Okay, that's a lie, but they are operated by remote-control these days. Magee also gives us an unofficial study of just who is likely to buy such expensive meat-cooking equipment. They're called *redneckosexuals*—distant cousin of the north's metrosexual—and chances are that you, too, have one in your family. But the fork doesn't stop there. John T. Edge, the Southern food guru, visits a country juke outside Amite, Louisiana, to experience the delicacy of eating pig lips fresh out of the packing plant. It takes him about four beers to muster the courage, and all the while we are treated to insider information on the processing of pig parts. It's a testament to our region's tough character, evident in the title, "I'm Not Leaving Until I Eat This Thing."

Following this is Lisa Daily's personal account of a frantic race to buy a house in the South—well, Florida, to be exact. An expert on dating and relationships, Daily focuses on the new topic of real estate in order to teach us all the valuable lesson that it takes more than a man shower, faux fireplace, and the theme from *Rhinestone Cowboy* to make a house a home.

Host of the wonderful *Thacker Mountain Radio* show, Jim Dees gives us a naked, muddy exploration of that epic, inexhaustible literary subject: fishing. Likely Dees had *Moby-Dick* in mind as he conjured his own version of the great white whale—a Mississippian named Skip who weighs an "eighth of a ton" and angles in the nude. If you haven't heard Dees' quick wit on the radio, this story is just a small taste of what you're missing.

And rounding out this anthology, though certainly not least among its offerings, is the romantic, riotous, and tearfully funny tale of "Sally the Screamer." A chapter originally banned by the publisher from his latest book, this classic Ed Williams piece shows the notorious "Brotherhood" at it again in Juliette, Georgia. This love story involving Ed's aging father and his squeeze, Sally, will have you howling right along with its unchecked passion and hysterical barnyard noises, and it provides the perfect, tender ending that any book of humor deserves.

In closing, I'll stop just short of calling *Southern Fried Farce* the best anthology of all time. Perhaps a more realistic aspiration is that this book will prove we "Suthnus" are indeed as hilarious as we often credit ourselves; that in this modern era, we can still devise elaborate spoofs to the high degree of our literary predecessors; and that we still have the awareness to mock both our real and stereotyped provinciality, even in spite of urbanization and globalization—two words we have only begun to spell, much less comprehend.

But regardless of the expectations and assumptions surrounding this and every anthology, if you take one thing away from this book, I hope it is a stomach ache from laughing too hard.

Now on with the show...

Henry Oehmig
September 2007
Chattanooga, Tennessee

Sex Devil

Jack Pendarvis

Gentlemen:

I would like to give you my idea for one of your comic books. Well it is not one of your comic books yet, but it soon will be! I call my idea Sex Devil.

Sex Devil starts out as a normal high school student. Unfortunately his fellow classmates do not think he is normal. For you see, Sex Devil (real name Randy White) has a cleft palate.

Sex Devil attempts to get his fellow classmates to like him. Unfortunately he pretends that he knows karate, which is a lie. Sex Devil's lies are soon discovered. After that his fellow classmates put a thing on the blackboard. It is a picture of Sex Devil (I mean Randy White) with slanting eyes, which he does not have. Underneath the picture it says Wandy Wite, Kawate Kiwwah. Also there is a bubble coming out of Randy White's mouth. Randy White is saying WAH!

A school janitor sees Randy White's humiliation. After school the janitor who is Asian American pulls Randy White to the side. Randy White is apprehensive yet he follows the school janitor to his creepy shack. Underground beneath the shack there is a training facility for a rare form of karate called Jah-Kwo-Ton. Randy White goes there every day and learns how to fight Jah-Kwo-Ton style which nobody else in America knows except the janitor.

The janitor has vowed not to fight because he accidentally killed a man once. He has also made Randy White swear not to defend the janitor in case anything happens to him. The janitor has learned to accept his fate.

One day the same classmates who pick on Randy White accidentally kill the janitor. Well it is partially on purpose and partially on accident. Randy White attempts to aid the janitor but the janitor tells him to remember his vow. Randy White remembers his vow. Now his classmates assume that Randy White is more cowardly than ever.

Now we go forward into the future. Sex Devil can afford the right kind of medical insurance to where his cleft palate can be surgically fixed. While he is pretending to be Randy White he continues to talk like he has a cleft palate. This is just to conceal his secret identity.

All of the boys of Sex Devil's high school class have grown into manhood to become a criminal organization. They run the city under cover of darkness, plotting fake terrorist plots to keep the city in turmoil while they make their robberies. As a result some innocent Arab Americans get sent to prison.

Sex Devil is the prison psychiatrist for the innocent Arab Americans. They can tell that Sex Devil is their friend. The Arab Americans instruct Sex Devil in the ways of a secret cult to where Sex Devil now has ultimate control over his body. Now Sex Devil is an expert in two different secret cults of ancient lore. He is also a trained psychiatrist with mastery over the human mind. No one can match his prowess based on his unique balance of science, skill and sorcery.

Sex Devil finds out from the Arab Americans that the very same people who framed them are the same people who used to pick on Sex Devil all the time. Sex Devil vows revenge.

One night he goes undercover at the chemical factory of his old enemy, who now goes by the name of Black Friday. In the middle of a fight where Black Friday unfairly uses guns Sex Devil gets chemicals spilled on his genital region. Black Friday uses the opportunity to get away.

Sex Devil retreats to his underground lair, which is located beneath the janitor shack. He examines his genital region and discovers that his genital region now has amazing powers. Combined with the bodily control he has learned from the Arab Americans now Sex Devil realizes he has a unique opportunity.

Sex Devil starts out by dating Black Friday's girlfriend. This is the same girl that used to make fun of Sex Devil but she doesn't know it is the same person because he talks completely different.

First Sex Devil takes Jennifer to a nice restaurant. Jennifer is impressed by Sex Devil's worldly manners. Because of his secret mastery of bodily control he is also the best dancer anyone has ever seen. It is the greatest date ever. Jennifer asks Sex Devil if he wants to come up for some coffee. Sex Devil jokes, who knows where that will lead. Sex Devil leaves politely without taking advantage of Jennifer.

When Sex Devil gets home he has about six or seven phone calls from Jennifer on his answering machine. Please Sex Devil, I need to see you.

Sex Devil goes back over to Jennifer's apartment. On the way he stops and buys some flowers. Then he climbs up a drainpipe and enters Jennifer's bedroom.

Jennifer thanks Sex Devil for the flowers. They are so beautiful Sex Devil. Black Friday never buys me flowers. Sex Devil says enough of this talk. Then Sex Devil and Jennifer have intimacy.

Black Friday wonders what is wrong with Jennifer. She seems to be distracted all the time. He does not know she is secretly thinking of her intimacy with Sex Devil. Jennifer refuses to have intimacy with Black Friday. Intimacy with Black Friday has become hollow. Nothing can compare to the amazing powers of Sex Devil's genital region.

Black Friday becomes depressed. Black Friday loses his ability to have intimacy. He must see a psychiatrist. Get me the best psychiatrist in the city! Little does he realize it is Sex Devil.

Black Friday unburdens the problems of his soul to Sex Devil. On the outside Sex Devil is concerned. On the inside Sex Devil is ha ha ha!

Black Friday can no longer do his criminal activities because he has lost all worth of himself as a human being. Black Friday can no longer perform intimacy because of his crippling depression. Every time Black Friday leaves the house Sex Devil comes over and has intimacy with Jennifer. Please Sex Devil I love you, can't we get married? No Jennifer, I am married to my work.

At the end of the first issue Black Friday falls off a cliff. Now Sex Devil must go to work on the rest of the class. At the end of every issue one of Sex Devil's fellow classmates falls off a cliff or is caught in the gears of a large machine or blows themself up in an explosion or capsizes or a similar disaster. Or they are in a submarine that slowly fills up with water. It is never Sex Devil's fault but he doesn't feel bad about it because they are getting what they deserve. Every time Jennifer is like please won't you spend the whole night Sex Devil? What is with all this wham bam thank you mam? And Sex Devil is like maybe some other time baby. Because Sex Devil has more important things on his mind. And Jennifer is like I am starting to think you are just using me for intimacy like a hor. And Sex Devil is like now you are getting the picture baby.

In conclusion I hope you will start making the comic book Sex Devil because it deals with issues that young people care about today.

Down in Mexico with Vic, Big Vicious, and Bernadette

Clyde Edgerton

Vic and I stop at a little side-street grocery store in the village of Zapata, southwest Mexico, near the Pacific coast. It's February, dry season, and dusty, but almost everywhere we've seen red Indian Spring flowers.

Outside the grocery's wide, open doorway sits a wooden barrel full of brooms, handles down, and just inside the door are waist high fruit bins. The smells are sweet: cantaloupes, tiny bananas, mangos, and papayas. A "reacher"—a two-fingered metal hand on the end of a broomstick—retrieves goods from top shelves. Anybody can use it.

We've been fly fishing on Rio Agua Caliente. The riverbanks, in contrast to a gray dusty countryside, are plush with dark green plants and weeping willow trees. The water is as clear as fresh air.

Before fishing, we managed to get our rental car stuck in sand near the river. A friendly Mexican holding a machete walked across the shallow riverbed and helped us push the car onto firm ground. In Spanish, Vic joked with our rescuer, Miguel. Later, when we returned to our car from fishing—no luck—Miguel sat in the river, bathing; a little board rested on the riverbank holding his soap and shampoo.

I pay for our goods at the grocery store. Vic makes the woman behind the counter laugh. Vic Miller makes everybody laugh.

My wife's Uncle Duke owns a villa—a *casita*—at Careyes, a few miles north of Zapata. Careyes, a place where grass and plants are green from automatic sprinklers, and seaside the apartments and houses are brightly multi-colored. Duke is generous to friends and family—my family is vacationing in his casita and an adjoining one belonging to a friend of his. I figured way back when we were invited that if I could get Vic down here, just sort of turn him loose with his fly rods, snorkeling gear, maps, walking shoes, his rise-and-shine-let's-jump-off-something-today energy, with his few lives left from the starting nine, then something interesting might happen. Besides, I hadn't seen him in a few years. He'd been with the Kuna Indians in Panama, anchored just off shore, living on his sailboat.

*

I met Vic in his hometown, Albany, Georgia, fifteen years ago. I was there to read at the local library, and he was showing me around town. In a bar he told me this story:

Vic, his friend Fred, Fred's two kids, and the kids' white poodle were all driving along in Fred's station wagon in a downpour when the dog's collar got hung on a window handle in back. Vic tried to help the dog get loose and the dog snapped at him. Vic already had a secret, strong dislike of the dog. One of the kids then tried to help the dog and accidentally rolled him over so that the collar tightened, and the dog stopped breathing and went limp—with his eyes kind of bugged out. The kids started screaming. Fred pulled over to the side of the road. Vic got the dog off the window handle (easier this time), out of the car into the pouring rain and handed him to Fred, who'd also stepped outside.

The kids are in the car, still screaming, noses pressed to the window. Fred hands the dog back to Vic and says, "Bring him back to life. You know how to do it." Vic once brought a dog back to life with mouth-to-mouth resuscitation, and Fred knew about it.

Vic wouldn't take the dog. He stepped back and said, "You can do it as good as I can." Vic was glad the dog was dead, see. "Just cradle him in your arms, hold his mouth closed, blow in through his nose, wait a few seconds, then blow again."

By now Fred's comb-over was down over one ear and his glasses were all fogged up and he was standing in the rain with this limp dog and the kids' crying faces were still pressed to the window.

He cradles the dog, grabs its snout, covers it with his mouth and blows. The little dog swells up. Fred stops blowing. The dog goes down. He blows again. The dog swells up. Backs off. Dog goes down. Up. Down. Suddenly, the dog starts squirming, then wiggling, and in no time is as good as new.

A couple of years later I incorporated the story into a novel I was writing. I didn't bother to ask Vic. In fact, I hadn't seen or heard from Vic since that library visit.

My galleys to the novel came to me just before a reading in Atlanta, Georgia. I read the story to a book conference audience and after the reading a sprite, elderly woman came up to me and said, "I read that same story in a magazine. It was written by Vic Miller."

What the hell? "Would you know how to get in touch with him?" I asked her.

"No. But I'll be happy to find out."

"That would be great."

She sent me Vic's address and phone number. I called him.

"Vic. Clyde Edgerton here. We met a few years ago in Albany. I was there for a reading."

"Oh yes. I remember."

"Do you remember the story you told me about your friend Fred bringing that little poodle back to life?"

"Sure do."

"I was thinking about using that story in a novel I'm writing, and I wonder if that'd be okay with you."

"By all means. I'd be honored. I wrote it up already, but you go right ahead."

Vic then invited my daughter and me to accompany him and his daughter to swim with the manatees near Crystal River, Florida. We accepted, and Vic and I have been adventuring together ever since.

Vic quotes Shakespeare, Keats and his friends. He's had

one successful and one unsuccessful heart operation, he's sixty-something, not sure that he wants another operation if it'll slow him down and thus tends to live every day as his last. He's strong, bull-headed at times, laid-back most of the time, curious about most anything, full of stories and blessed with many friends. He will teach any stranger about fly fishing, about fossils, arrowheads—instruct and explain with the patience of a rested mother. This is one reason I hope he's around for my two-year-old, Nathaniel, as he grows up—he reminds me of one of my own long gone favorite uncles. He's been bruised and stitched up after all sorts of encounters, several with crocodiles and wild boars. He fought a bull in a carnival bullring in Spain, and lost. Early in his life he was a "cave diver."

Vic recently sailed his forty-four foot sailboat back to the states from Panama, where he enjoys the company of the Kuna Indians, entertains them, eats their food and celebrates with them. He's now visiting his hometown, Albany, Georgia, for a while but will return to the Indians after putting up with as much American life as he can handle. He likes the way the Kuna live, the way they treat their children and each other. He's trying to develop a commercial market for their ancient *mola*, a layered tapestry of artistic designs.

Vic tells of an early encounter with the Kuna: He and the chief, Brown, were talking, and Vic noticed that Brown kept scratching his arm. Vic offered Neosporin. The chief used it and then took off his shirt and asked Vic to apply some to his back. Soon a group of Indians were lined up for his "magical" medication. Vic ran out of Neosporin, and to continue to please them, reverted to dabs of toothpaste. They came to trust him and like him, love him I'm sure, and he set anchor.

Before returning to the states, Vic killed a crocodile that was eating the villagers' dogs. He kept the croc and tried without success to get the Indians to eat the delicious crocodile meat. The chief awarded Vic a necklace made from two teeth and a part of the spine of the crocodile. For Vic, it is sacred, and represents his tie to a people he respects and admires.

*

Vic and I return to the casita with the groceries and find out that an ocean fishing trip has been scheduled for the next morning. That night we sit around the dinner table, talking and laughing and mostly listening to and watching Vic—my wife Kristina, Nathaniel, Kristina's mother and father: Hannah and P.M, her sister, Merritt, a family friend Maggie, and me. Some of Vic's stories I've heard, but like a fine, old ballad, a good, well-told story works over and over.

*

The fishing guide's name is Sergio, and he and Vic talk fishing, weather and ocean tides in Spanish. Along with us is my father-in-law, P. M.

We're in a twenty-foot motorboat trolling with heavy duty rods and reels less than a quarter of a mile from shore. The coast is mostly rocky bluff with occasional sandy beaches and palms. Swells move into the crevices, and plumes of water shoot up like geysers. Waterfalls are left as swells recede.

Headed south along the rocky seashore, near Careyes, we pass an estate high on a cliff. A round tower up there reminds Vic of a story. (Five random objects on a table would remind Vic of five stories.) A round tower in Costa Rica was once rented out by the owner, Vic's friend, as a honeymoon suite. A pet parrot lived in the tower and would occasionally fly through an open window into the dining room and perch, sit a while and then sing, "Ooooohh, ahhhh, yes, yes, yes."

A fishing reel suddenly whines, the rod bends. P. M. brings in the fish, a species of tuna that Sergio says we should throw back because the meat is too dark. Vic protests. We'll keep the fish and cook it, he says.

We'll catch two more fish on our half-day outing: another locally unfit tuna and a jack. Back at the casita, Vic will fillet the two tuna, cut the fillets into chunks and fry them in a spicy flour and cornmeal mix. Next day he'll convert a large flowerpot into a smoker and smoke the jack.

The tuna *was* pretty dark. I can understand why the locals don't eat them. The smoked jack was delicious.

*

On the fifth day, Merritt suggests a group hike at Turtle Beach, several miles away. She drives Vic, Maggie and me to a narrow dirt road exiting Route 200, marked with a hand-written sign: "Polo." We continue along the narrow road through thick, gnarled, scrub oaks and underbrush to a fork—"Polo" to the left.

We go right and finally emerge on a wide grass and sand plain that leads to a magnificent, crescent-shaped beach at least three miles long with rock outcroppings at each end. No humans, no structure in sight. We decide that the beach's beauty surely dooms it to be a future resort spot. We decide to walk to the northern end of the beach where there may be a creek for fly fishing. Vic has brought snorkeling and fly fishing gear.

The beach is high, wide and level, but then slants downward to where very tall, powerful waves are breaking in close, throwing tons of water rapidly up the incline and, in places, onto the flat top of the beach. The water then rushes back down the incline creating a terrific undertow. The middle and upper parts of the tall waves are light green and translucent.

Right away we see a lone, baby sea turtle headed across the beach for the water, something we've all seen in films but few have seen in real life. We scan for others but there are none. We follow him along. He makes it to the wet sand on the long downhill incline, is twice washed back ten or fifteen feet by the surf. We refuse to help him—he will need the strength he's building. Finally he's picked up and sucked out to sea.

We continue north. Vic looks for fossils, quietly and patiently scratching with a stick in the sand.

Merritt points north. "Something just ran into the ocean."

"Probably the way the water was breaking," I say. "That's a powerful undertow."

"No, it was something alive. It looked like a log."

We continue north. In a minute I see the log. "It was a log," I say. I figure it washed back onto shore. Suddenly it rises on four short, stubby legs and runs into the ocean.

"Crocodile!" says Vic. It's as if he were struck by lightning. He is new. He grabs his flippers and mask, heads for the water. "They think you can't see them underwater," he says over his shoulder. "That's the best place to catch them. Won't this be something for Nathaniel!" My two-year-old son.

Merritt points again. "There it is." The croc is floating about forty feet out, nose and eyes above water, just beyond the breakers. The water is so clear you can see the rest of her. She appears to be a little over a yard long. Vic calls out, "Hang on, Bernadette, I'm coming to get you, sweetheart."

A big wave knocks Vic on his ass, throws him underwater, out of sight until he appears—rolling in the surf. I notice that he stays relaxed, doesn't fight the water.

"Big Vicious," says Maggie. "He's in a wrestling match with Big Vicious."

Vic charges in again, manages somehow to stumble at the base of a high breaker and then dive beneath it. He surfaces beyond the breakers and swims toward where we last saw the croc. But Bernadette is gone.

We walk along the beach looking for Bernadette in the water. Vic searches beyond the waves, face down in the water; he finally gives up and is washed in to us. We decide we might see Bernadette on our trip back from the north end.

"It's pretty simple," says Vic. "You just catch them around the neck where they can't get their teeth back to you. And then grab that tail and get it under your arm, so they can't get all that torque going. They've got *some* torque."

As we walk north we notice a swamp, about three hundred yards from the ocean. It's Bernadette's home, probably. As we approach we see a pond with brackish, brown water bordering the swamp. Vic unpacks fly fishing gear and we begin fishing. Merritt and Maggie continue walking north along the beach. We hear the waves thundering on the beach.

When it's finally clear we're not likely to catch fish, we walk back toward the ocean, headed toward the north end of the beach. The surf is significantly rougher than it was earlier.

On the sand, not far from the breakers, I look behind us and there, a hundred yards or so back, resting on the beach near the top of the long incline down from the flat beach, is Bernadette—or a log.

"Vic. There's Bernadette. Or a log."

Vic looks. He crouches. He's new again.

At this spot on the beach, where we are—but not back where Bernadette is—the tide has washed a four or five foot vertical wall into the sand. Vic slides down it, gets as close to the water as possible, and starts creeping toward Bernadette. He moves slowly, like a cat. But the surf, even knee deep, is powerful enough to stagger him. When he's about fifty yards from Bernadette, she turns and skitters into the water. Vic walks back to me, and we move away from the water to the top of the flat beach, out of sight of where Bernadette will, we hope, come back to rest. And from where she will surely watch for baby sea turtles. Or Vic.

We wait five minutes or so, and sneak back to where we can see. Bernadette is back.

"There's that big washed up stump above where she is," I say. "Why don't we just go on down to the stump—she can't see us from there—and then we charge. I mean, and then you charge."

"She'll outrun us. They're fast as hell. But only for short distances. The only way to catch her is cut her off from the ocean—come in from the ocean. That's what I need to do. And you be ready on the beach in case she heads for the swamp. They won't attack unless they're cornered. You don't have to worry about that. Just have a stick to hold her off, in case."

"In case of what?"

"I don't know. Just in case."

I'm thinking, He's going to try to make it out through that impossible surf and then come in on Bernadette back through that impossible surf—maybe washing up right on top of her.

Bernadette rests at the far reach of the wash, just below the crest of the beach.

"I don't think you can make it out through that surf," I say. "It's rougher than it was an hour ago."

Vic is donning snorkeling equipment. Not listening to me. I've seen him get an undeniable notion from time to time.

Maggie and Merritt are walking toward us from the north. I point south. They understand and move away from the water so Bernadette won't see them.

Vic tries to make it into the ocean. He's rebuffed violently. Big Vicious simply knocks his feet out from under him and sucks him into the base of a breaking wave, and he's washed back up onto the beach. He tries again—same thing. He's shaken. He walks to me and stands, dripping and thinking. Merritt and Maggie are nearby, watching. Bernadette apparently can't see us this far away. I know Vic well enough to know he's going to try again no matter what I—or anyone—says.

But I want to go on record. "I wouldn't do it, Vic. It's too rough."

No response. He's putting on the damn flippers.

We've discussed what I'm supposed to do: cut off Bernadette if she heads for the swamp. I imagine her coming over the crest of the beach, headed toward me. I imagine myself racing toward the car with her at my heels, snapping.

As Vic starts for the ocean I start up the beach toward Bernadette, but out of her sight. I'm thinking, I will not wait here, because if Vic starts to drown, I may go in after him, and if Vic can't handle the surf I know I can't. We'll both drown.

I don't want to drown, so I keep walking south toward Bernadette. It hits me: if I were in trouble, Vic would come after me, and if he gets in trouble, he'll probably be washed in close enough to pull out. I stop and turn.

He's made it beyond the waves. I walk slowly south as he swims in the same direction beyond the breakers. The waves come as great swells, and Vic is riding the swells, swimming as I walk.

I get to the stump and stop. Vic is almost straight out from me. I picture Bernadette resting between us. Facing me.

The crest of sand allows me to see the ocean far out, but only the tops of the waves close to shore. I hear the ka-plooms of their breaking on the beach. I wait. Vic turns toward me and starts swimming in. He's wearing the goggles, and the snorkel is in his mouth; his head is above water as the swells bring him in. He seems relaxed, calm. I give him a thumbs up. He responds. Now he's closer so that he bobs up into sight at the top of a swell and then out of sight. I've got to get my timing right. I will be able to see when he's on his last swell just before it breaks, and then I'll have to pause, then walk toward the ocean. If Bernadette sees me before seeing Vic, she'll have a too early jump toward the ocean. Vic's job is to cut her off and pounce on her. Somehow. My job is to watch.

Vic is at the top of a swell, in sight. Down, out of sight. Up. He's on the wave that will break. He and the wave disappear; I hear the "boom" of the crashing wave. I pause: thousand one, thousand two, thousand three. I walk toward the ocean. Suddenly I see only Vic's head and shoulders above the sand crest. He's running, dodging, head-faking like a man after a chicken. He dives. Over the crest I see the surf and Vic, on his knees, pressing Bernadette's neck and tail into the sand. He stands, staggers in the surf, walks toward me with the prize.

"My mask!" he yells. I look. Flippers, mask and snorkel are being sucked into the ocean. I go after them. I manage to retrieve the floating flippers. But the mask and snorkle are gone.

Back up on the beach, I get a close look at Bernadette. She looks like...well, like a crocodile.

I see how Vic is holding her. "Get your rods and stuff,"

I say. "I'll carry her to the car." Hell, I ain't afraid of a little crocodile.

"Be sure you hold the tail."

I take her. She's heavier than she looks. Her eyes are eerie—so clear, like green-gray glass reflecting light. I turn her on her side. She's very relaxed. The lid closes over the eye on top.

"I want you to be the one to take her in and show her to Nathaniel," says Vic. "We can put her in the swimming pool, get a leash. Then we can bring her back tonight."

My arms are so tense they begin to go numb, and I start to hand Bernadette back to Vic, carefully.

"She seems dead almost," I say.

"She's not that. They'll play possum on you. You know, a possum faints though. She's not fainted. She's just waiting for us to relax."

We wrap her in t-shirts—she seems to be asleep—and start the drive home. Vic holds her. Merrit and Maggie ask Vic crocodile questions, and he answers with stories.

We reach the gate, the checkpoint. A man inside a white truck sits near the gate. I throw up my hand. He nods and waves us through.

Back at the casita, Vic insists that I carry Bernadette in to Nathaniel. I refuse. Nathaniel will see the true catcher holding the caught. Everybody inside is astounded. Especially Nathaniel.

Vic places Bernadette into the little swimming pool and gets in with her. This is not quite the modeling behavior I want for Nathaniel, is it? But on the other hand…in a few years

I'll tell Nathaniel this story and let him know that without Uncle Vic, our trip would have been far less memorable, and if Nathaniel is lucky he'll get to spend more time with Uncle Vic and see what it's like to live a day like it's your last.

The Wrestler and the Fan

Celia Rivenbark

I remember just like it was yesterday the sticky July morning I stole the wrestling poster off the telephone pole and made little Hermie Drucker cry.

Sure, I was 12 and I should've taken the high road. Hermie, the asthmatic, red-headed kid brother of a friend of mine, was only 7, and the wail he let out when he pedaled his Western Auto banana bike up to that pole to claim "his" poster could've been heard six counties away.

I could easily hear Hermie's screams of outrage from my post across the road at MacMillan's, a rickety country store with a wood floor so worn out that, to a bare foot, it felt as soft as a satin bedspread. Watching Hermie from underneath the rusty overhang at the Sinclair pumps made me feel a little guilty.

There he was, so full of hope and determination, ready to rip "our" poster off that telephone pole and skedaddle back home, where he would have, no doubt, taped it to his wall right alongside the Rip Hawk and Swede Hansen poster he'd stolen from me not six months earlier.

Just thinking about it made me mad as a hen on a hot griddle. Little shit, I thought to myself, picturing the way the green and orange and yellow striped poster *with photos* would have looked on my own bedroom wall.

Hermie and I both wanted this latest poster, and we finally agreed (me, with my fingers crossed neatly behind my back) that the only Christian thing to do would be to wait until the tag-team match between George Becker and Johnny Weaver at the Wallace National Guard Armory was officially over. Which had been last night.

"You snooze, you lose," I shouted to Hermie, who just stared at me as if I had sprouted horns and a forked tail. All that was left on the creosote pole were little bitty pieces of the orange corners of the poster stuck to a few staples that I hadn't been able to dislodge. They mocked him.

Although he was only 7 years old, Hermie's apple hadn't fallen far from the evangelistic family tree. His grandmother, a snow-haired woman of four feet eight inches in height and the same approximate width, had taught the Catechism to all the country kids in our dinky little Carolina town.

"You're going to Hell!" Hermie said, now wiping away the beginnings of a tear.

As he stomped his flip-flopped foot pointlessly into a growth of pop-gums, I watched with increasing amusement, finally catching his eye just long enough to flip him off.

"Hell! Hell! That there just seals the deal!" Hermie hollered.

I'd have to do a good deal of Catechism refreshment for loving Hermie's misery so much.

"We had a deal!" he yelled with a fierceness I wasn't altogether expecting. Hanging at his sides, Hermie's fat little fists were balled up so tight it made the freckles disappear right off his knuckles.

I cupped my hand behind my ear and shook my head. I can't hear a word out of your freckly-lipped mouth, I was letting him know. Which, obviously, wasn't the truth at all.

"What's up Hermie's butt?" my friend Deb asked, having maneuvered her bike under the overhang beside mine.

"I got the poster first," I said.

"Don't look like he's taking it too good," she said, causing us both to laugh because now Hermie had taken to jumping up and down on the pop-gums like a damn fool.

"It's mighty hot out, Hermie," I hollered. Deb ripped open a skinny little sleeve of Lance's salted peanuts and, just as we'd done a million times before, poured half the contents of the bag into her Co-Cola and handed me the rest. We switched off and shared like that, first me buying the peanuts and then Deb. This was a concept Hermie was going to have to learn the hard way.

"Shut up!" he said, continuing to stomp and getting redder and redder in the face.

I wasn't sure if 7-year-olds could actually have a stroke, but Hermie looked like he was headed that way.

"Both of y'all need to grow up," said Deb, wiping some stray peanut salt off her cheeks with the back of her hand. "It's just a stupid wrestling match. Who cares anyway?"

WHO CARES???

Deb, dressed in a ruffly midriff shirt and madras shorts she'd bought with money from priming tobacco, had no time for such pursuits. At 14, she was far more interested in finding a boyfriend with a car who she could go "ridin' around" with on Friday night. This is what passed for entertainment back in rural Eastern North Carolina in the 60s and 70s, and may still, for all I know.

Maybe wrestling was something I'd grow out of, but I doubted it. My idea of a good time had nothing to do with getting in some fool's car and riding around the Dairi-O something like 700 times in a row while Steppenwolf howled from the 8-track.

No, when I was 12, a good time was defined by eating an entire box of Crackin' Good butter cookies (always on sale at Winn Dixie for 59 cents a box) while watching the wrestling matches on TV every Saturday night.

It should be noted that no one in my family shared my passion for wrestling. In fact, the only person in my immediate world who understood how I felt about wrestling was, at this very minute, seated on a tuffet made of stomped pop-gums, crying his little heart out.

Looking at the broken little boy, I felt like a monster.

A monster with the coolest damn poster of them all. Because I loved George Becker and Johnny Weaver better than all the other professional wrestlers put together. There had been brief flirtations with others, but George and Johnny were my favorites, and nothing would ever change that.

I wasn't alone in my obsession, else how could they have raised so many thousands of dollars from truly poor people who would stand in line more than an hour to sit in the sweaty, smelly Armory? Usually it was a fund-raiser with a smallish percentage going to the volunteer fire department to buy a Jaws of Life or maybe the Ruritans' building fund, so you could even say that it was noble to attend these events. Not so noble, perhaps, to shotgun beers out in the parking lot ahead of time like some of the kids did, but nothing's perfect.

I wasn't old enough to go to a wrestling match at the Armory by myself, so I had to settle for watching my heroes on TV. When that nasty little Japanese wrestler (I forget his name on purpose) took out a drawstring bag of salt hidden in the waistband of his shorts and tossed the contents into George and Johnny's eyeballs, I jumped up from my chair, scattering flower-shaped butter cookies all over the oval braided rug on our living room floor.

"Y'all know he's sneaky!" I'd shout, talking to the TV just as if my boys could hear me and correct their behavior.

"Educated people don't watch this sort of thing," my mother huffed as she walked by and scowled at the cookies on the rug. "You know it's all fake, don't you?"

I had an answer for that awful question right ready.

"If it's fake, then why does Dr. Dawes believe in it enough

to buy out 50 front row seats every single time the wrestling comes to the Armory?"

My mother shook her head. She didn't have an answer for that, and, frankly, no one else did either.

Dr. Dawes was as close as you could get to a real, live saint walking and living amongst us. He healed people and saved lives and birthed so many thousands of babies (me included) that he was even written up as "Tar Heel of the Week" in the *Raleigh News & Observer*.

"You think the Tar Heel of the Week wouldn't know if something was fake or not?" I asked, sensing that I'd found the perfect vulnerable spot.

My mother shrugged sadly and left the room, unable to offer any sort of rational explanation for this man she loved and respected being caught up in something so obviously moronic.

But there sat Dr. Dawes at ringside—I saw it with my own eyes one night when I was in my 20s—the same scrupulously clean and oddly elegant hands that had caught thousands of babies and comforted thousands more sick souls, clenched into fists balled up just like little Hermie Drucker's on that long-ago day. At 75 or so, Dr. Dawes shouted, slung popcorn, and all but crawled into the ring himself to right a perceived wrong.

"Settle down now, Doc," the referee said, trying unsuccessfully not to grin. No doubt, Dr. Dawes had delivered the referee into the world along with anyone else under about the age of 50 that happened to be in the audience.

In the newspaper, it had been noted that Dr. Dawes had

"even delivered three sets of Siamese twins!" This was, of course, before political correctness would water that down to the clinical "conjoined twins" that is used today. Face it: When the bad-guy wrestler in the ring with an Asian heritage is nicknamed "The Yeller Menace," it's fairly obvious that no one frets much about racial stereotypes.

The stereotypes were in glorious form in the wrestling ring. Maybe that was the appeal of the whole thing to someone like me who liked everything simple and orderly. The good guys looked good, and the bad guys wore hideous tight masks over their faces and scowled and spat. Good looks helped. Over the years, I switched my shallow loyalties to a wrestler named Mike Rotundo, who I once drove 100 miles to see in person at somebody else's crappy National Guard Armory.

Years later, long after little Hermie Drucker had become a highway patrolman much respected by all of the community and I had become a newspaper reporter not respected by much of anybody, I had the chance to go to a wrestling match again. I'd volunteered to do a profile on the state of rural wrestling fund-raisers, arguing that they were practically non-existent thanks to cable. I'd done something similar on womanless weddings and on people who make clothes out of beer cans and a whole bunch of other Southern anomalies.

"Maybe nobody goes anymore because they finally figured out that it's all fake," said one snooty reporter who had moved south from Connecticut. "It's not like it's a real sport." He put little quote marks in the air when he got to the word *sport*.

I chuckled at the image of what this annoying-ass Yankee

boy would look like after a few seconds in the ring with my old crush, Mike Rotundo. Stewed squash, that's what.

Showing up with pad and pen, I was going to do something that I was doing a lot of lately, much to the delight of all the Yankee transplants, and that was to tell them about the way it used to be.

Stepping into a pitiful gym with peeling paint, 38 miles from the nearest Starbucks, I watched a young local make his debut in the ring.

He called himself Mean Mike Brash. Trouble was, he wasn't mean at all. Just a very young, pale, and rather slightly built blonde-headed boy who thought high school was overrated and was chasing his dream right off the TV screen and into this dilapidated gym. It was for a good cause, as usual. In this case, charity began, and ended, at home. Proceeds would help buy paint for the gym.

Thank goodness, his tag-team partner, The Dark Knight, was more savvy. He played to the crowd, pretending to throw a chair at a little girl who screamed and hid behind her 18-year-old daddy's skinny legs.

Once the match started, with the good guys wearing red, white, and blue and Mean Mike calling a little bent-over country woman who was booing him from the front row "you toothless ol' hag," I felt right at home.

It had been too long. I forgot about taking notes, savoring the spectacle in front of me and burning my throat with too-salty popcorn.

The little woman balled up her fists in front of her face,

just like Dr. Dawes had done so many years ago, and, to the amazement of everyone in the gym except her grown son beside her, invited Dark Knight to "come down 'ere and say that, you bastard!"

Fake? Real? It mattered not. This was Southern-style wrestling at its essence. And I, for one, knew that the only thing that would make this night more perfect would be a box of butter cookies to eat or perhaps to toss into the ring in disgust.

I heard that Mean Mike's career ended shortly after that night, having had to choose between snapping necks and saving souls. He became a gospel singer with a band that played in the very same Armories where he'd once called nice people's grandmas toothless ol' hags.

Only in the South, I thought. Happily.

The Delicate Lives of Amphibians

George Singleton

Only because my father's best friend got caught running a makeshift and subterranean hoochie-coochie show down in the work bay of his ancient Gulf station, his patrons lolling around ground-level while the half-stripped girl danced atop scattered cat litter to soak up oil, plus dirty red rags, and the occasional misplaced socket wrench or screwdriver—*only* because someone went outside the local sheriff's department and told on Mr. Jervey in such an obstinate and determined way that state investigators got involved—did I *almost* get caught illegally depleting the perhaps-protected salamander population of the North and South Carolina border where we lived. I mean, I got caught—which would've never happened hadn't Mr. Jervey attracted attention in his way, but I didn't get in trouble. Patrons of the gas station craned their necks into the hole, hooting, floating dollar bills down to the woman I'd snuck a peek at twice before. No one paid attention to me standing there with a cooler of redback, dusky, spring, longtailed, or blackbelly salamanders, ready to sell for bait to men who had no obvious jobs or hobbies beyond watching poor mountain girls tease them from below, or fishing. My father wasn't present on the day of Mr. Jervey's arrest—they arrested the girl, too, on charges of lewd behavior and indecent exposure—but it was my father's idea for me to always show up there on Friday afternoons in order to sell my bait. A deputy named Officer Durbin came up to me later as I stood there off to the side straddling my bike. He yelled something over his shoulder about how, if I were twenty feet closer, Jervey could've gotten charged with contributing to the delinquency of a minor.

I said, "My *daddy's* the one with the river rock business. I just catch the salamanders hiding beneath flat rocks. I'm not, technically, a miner."

Deputy Durbin looked in my cooler and said, "You Looper's boy? You little Stet Looper? You know you breaking a law. You know that, if we lived in the United States proper, I could arrest you for transporting rare and endangered habitat, or some such liberal notion."

I didn't cry. I said, catching on, "Good thing we live in South Carolina."

He smiled. He told me to run on home and take care of my three R's. "You take care of rod, rig, and reeling," he said. "I'll just keep a warning for you up here in my head. I got a whole list of all you little boys living up here in my head." He tapped his forehead.

I wasn't but ten years old, but I somehow I understood the notion of a misplaced modifier. What were little boys doing living inside the detective's head? Plus, there were no other kids up on the Unknown Branch of the Saluda River that I'd ever met. My father had to drive me ten miles sideways across a mountain on highway 11 to play catch with a boy who only had one arm. So the man was being hyperbolic, too. I think I was in college when my father called me up to tell me how this particular cop got arrested for being a pederast. So it was foreshadowing. I guess, looking back, I could tell people that I learned all of my needful English lessons from Officer Durbin.

I said, "Thank you, sir," because my father taught me early on how to talk to men wearing badges. When I was about three years old I confessed all my wrong-doings to Smokey Bear.

He patted me on top of my head softly about four hundred times, then told me to run on, which I did, the salamander bucket banging on my right knee-side. I'll admit that I couldn't shake the notion of the little boys living inside the cop's head. But seeing as tiny people lived inside the TV set and in the radio, maybe it was possible, I figured.

Anyway, let me say now that I never had a knack for capitalism. The salamander is a delicate little amphibian, and to keep them alive I had to rig an outdoor terrarium with a state-of-the-art filtration system. Selling each salamander for a dime apiece in 1979, I figured out about the time I took an economics class in college, might've made me a profit at about the turn of the century. Again, I was ten years old, which, according to my father, was three years past the age of when he was forced to work the river rock business for his father. After school I was supposed to stack what rocks got piled indiscriminately throughout the day on the banks of the Unknown Branch of the Middle Saluda River. I was to take flat change-purse-sized rocks to one pile, flat pancake-sized rocks to another pile, and—if I could lift them—anything larger onto a nearby pallet. It took about two days of my getting reprimanded by my father's lone employee, an old mountain drunk named Vickers, before I found ways to walk upriver with an old, metal, deep-green ammunition box, turn over rocks in the shallows, and grab what salamanders hid beneath. I averaged forty or fifty an afternoon.

"How many did you sell, Stet?" my father asked me when I returned from the crime scene. "I've been telling every landscaper who comes through buying rocks to tell his workforce about you. I haven't done any scientific surveys, but I believe that most men who work with river rocks on the land all week long, they get drawn to fishing on the weekends. I'm guessing you sold out."

We sat in the den-like space of our cabin-like house. It was more of a wooden warehouse where I grew up: two bedrooms on one end with a bathroom in the middle, two rooms on the other end with an added-on bathroom taking up half of what my mom used for a sewing room. Our den/living room/kitchen/dining room was all the same space. We used a wood stove that sat in the middle, surrounded with a homemade, welded barrier so no one stumbled onto it.

I said, "Mr. Jervey got arrested, I think. These cops took him away."

My father held his eyes wide toward me and didn't blink. Looking back at it all, I know that his face reddened out of embarrassment. I think my mother began humming. "I bet he pretended to sell oil that he wasn't really putting in engine blocks," my father said. "I bet he sold people recaps and told them they were new tires. I bet he didn't cotton to the expiration dates on the peanut butter crackers in his Lance machine. I bet his octane's not what he says it is." He hitched both sides of his blue cotton work pants. "I bet he's not adhering to federal guidelines vis-à-vis fluid disposal. I bet someone turned him in for selling car inspection stickers without conducting a full twelve-point inspection. I bet he's selling beer out of the back room. I bet he's selling beer on Sundays. I bet he's selling beer out of the back room to minors. On Sundays."

I could tell that my father wanted to keep me from talking. My mother looked up from her chair. "I bet he got caught for having a stripper perform on the premises without the requisite pasties or business license." Then she went back to etching fake fossils on flat rocks my father considered inferior—not passable even for a walkway between old buildings at a school for the blind. My mother used her engagement ring to cut her designs.

I said, "I didn't sell any salamanders. That's all I know,"

for I didn't want to tell on my dad and then get about the thirty-ninth lecture from him on how I'm to keep my mouth shut. I didn't want to get whipped from a spare leather belt that fit on his handmade, hand-operated dredge, either. I said, "Can I have a beer?"

"A perfect carboniferous fern fossil. Or is it the *skeleton* of a *brook trout*? This'll get me twenty dollars down at Dixie Rock and Gem," my mother said. She was the one in the family with a notion for economics.

Not that I knew anything about the extinction of delicate species, and not because I foresaw Jervey's Gulf closing down for good, thus leaving me without prospective bait buyers, but I got up from the floor, walked out on the porch, took my cooler of salamanders, and dumped them back into the Unknown Branch of the Middle Saluda River. It seemed the moral thing to do, here, in the midst of my curious and persistent parents. One day I might have to tell a badge-wearing authority about how I wasn't always a bad person.

My father joined me outside. He said, "You did good, Stet. Good job." He put his palm on the top of my head and left it there. I didn't tell him about Deputy Durbin kind of doing the same thing. "If we were Jewish I'd say that you were ready for a bar mitzvah. You're a man. You saw a naked woman, and you knew not to tell your mother about it. You're a chipped shard off an old piece of chalcedony."

Some of the salamanders darted down to the river bottom, covered themselves in silt, then scurried to a flat rock. Most of them floated downstream, belly up. I told my father that I didn't mean to kill them. I stood up and watched them wiggle and gyrate in the eddies—moving much like the naked woman in Mr. Jervey's gas station bay—and talked myself into believing that they, too, would come back into our lives, somehow, and repopulate this rock-laden, thrill-barren, unbalanced speck of unwritten laws.

Meow ... It's Happy Hour

Susan Reinhardt

My childhood never included lumbering, slobbering dogs, but instead was populated by at least a dozen cats, my favorite being Samantha, an adopted feline with a thirst for cheap booze.

When my parents flew to Spain for free—an indirect result of the cat and my father's regular Happy Hours—they asked if I'd keep her. I hesitated, knowing that Samantha required more attention and doting than bottle-feeding abandoned puppies.

"OK, I'll do it," I told Mama, who'd sacrificed her life for the needs of my sister and me and deserved this vacation. "Make sure you pack all her supplies and favorite beverages before dropping her off. I don't want my friends to see me in a liquor store buying fortified wine or Old Milwaukee."

"Well, when did we get so highfaluting?" she said, and I could hear the oven door slam and the sizzle of onions and butter on the stove, her nightly supper routine. "Don't worry. Y'all will get along just fine."

We'd never had a cat like Samantha. My dad loves to tell people how she came into our lives a hissing and back-arching wreck, and how with expensive cat food and twist-cap wine, she blossomed into a dream cat, the kind of pet every family longs to love.

He also tells people that if it weren't for Samantha, he'd be buried in the cold hard dirt as God intended and would be sitting in his green recliner instead of jetting off to foreign countries and ordering Mama not to pack seven suitcases.

"It's all that cat's fault we're going to Spain," Daddy said, growing pink about the face as the evening sun clocked out for the day and his second beer kicked in. "I spent $10,000 in a matter of two hours. I'm telling you, it's much easier to fork it out for big-ticket items when a few beers are under your belt. Opens the wallet right up."

Daddy never knew when he agreed to take on the orphaned animal, that she'd not only become his drinking buddy, but also the key reason he went for a burial upgrade.

*

Our lives began to change when my sister adopted an alcoholic cat resembling something pulled from a junkyard or tavern dumpster.

My mama knows not to bother Daddy until Happy Hour has loosened his shirt and inhibitions, and she used to go right along imbibing with him until she found Jesus and a few Bible verses at almost the exact same time her doctor discovered high blood pressure and a few benign lumps beneath her skin.

She decided to forgo that mellow feeling of being in the middle of one's second drink just as a warm sun is descending and life's sharp edges seem sandpapered and smoothed.

The cat took her place.

Samantha, who looked as if spawned from a pit bull, proved to be an alkie kitty from the time she was about six weeks old, having been raised in a frat house at the University of Georgia, where she awakened daily to feed upon fried chicken and mashed potato scraps along with keg beer. On special occasions she got margaritas or whatever concoction the frat guys had brewed to seduce sorority girls during the social mixers.

We inherited Sam because my younger sibling was a Little Sister at the frat house. At the end of college, sister Sandy packed all her belongings and waited on Daddy to drive up in his silver, pimp-mobile Cadillac with the U-haul attached to the back.

Sandy slid into the passenger seat, Samantha struggling and hissing in her arms.

"You're not considering bringing a cat home, young lady?" Daddy said, eyeing the scraggly, bleary-eyed creature. "That thing looks rabid."

"We can get it some shots," Sandy said. "It'll be left to die if—"

"Your mama already has two cats and isn't about to take one on that looks like it belongs in a feline rehab. Now run on back up to that big ol' fraternity house, and give it to one of those boys sitting by that keg on the porch."

Sandy hugged the cat close to her body. It attacked and behaved like a wild, cornered possum. "I can't," she said. "No one will take her but me."

"You're not going to be her saving grace and think you can—"

"Please, Daddy! I'll take care of her, and as soon as I get a job, it'll go off into the real world with me. Y'all won't have her but a few weeks, I'm sure."

Daddy has never been one to refuse my sister much. She has huge brown moose eyes and a supermodel's pout. She's tiny and butterfly-like in her movements, a graceful girl much unlike me. Whereas I chose to go into print media, she chose television for all the world to see and hear her charms.

My daddy saw the tears that sprang to Sandy's eyes (typically accompanied by her famous lip quiver). "Just a few weeks?" he said, staring at his daughter and the snarling cat.

"Thank you, thank you, thank you. I love you, Daddy. You're the best."

The drive from Athens, Georgia, to Spartanburg, South Carolina, was about two and a half hours. The cat moaned and howled, whined and emitted guttural sounds as if it were about to give birth or die on the spot. Daddy would glance over and see it trembling and fretting, an animal that seemed ready to jump straight out of its own mangy fur.

"What's wrong with that cat?" he asked, turning into a gas station just outside of Commerce, Georgia.

Sandy drew a deep breath and stared at Daddy for

a minute. "I forgot to tell you this one little thing." She scrunched up her cute little future anchorwoman face. "Sam's an alcoholic. We just need to get her a beer or two and—"

"Hey, now. Whoa. What did you say about this devil cat?"

"She drinks. And not like a lady. More like a three-fisted biker." Sandy couldn't help but laugh. Daddy couldn't help but cease respiration.

"Just go in," my sister said, "and get her an Old Milwaukee or some other $3 six-pack of beer. She's not picky about the brand."

My father seemed zombied, as if zapped with a tranquilizer gun. Sandy shook his shoulder. "Dad? A beer? It'll fix everything. You'll see. Look, I have Sam's saucer right here."

Daddy eased out of the long silver Cadillac and lifted the nozzle to fill the tank with mid-grade. The sun bore on his graying hair and closed eyes. After a few minutes, the nozzle clicked, and he put the hose back into place. Sandy rolled down the window. "Beer? Please?"

Dad walked into the convenience store and was gone for quite some time. When he returned, he carried a brown paper sack, the exact shape of a six-pack.

"It's Bud Lite," he said, getting behind the wheel. "You reckon she'll like it?"

"She's not picky. Once we get it in her, she'll quit shaking and start acting more like a nice kitty with dignity and manners."

My dad sort of shook his head. He's used to kooks in the family, having married a woman who has a wild sister, our Aunt Betty, who owned and harbored a pet skunk named Rosie.

At 70, Aunt Betty likes to do gymnastics and cut flips in

front of the preacher and anyone else who'll watch her land a perfect split.

"When she worked at the furniture store," Mama said, "She'd jump from bed to bed, and when customers came in, she'd hop off the sofas and do her air splits for them. She got more sales than any other person who ever worked there."

Aunt Betty paved the way for our family's quirks, so we owe her a debt of gratitude.

Sandy opened the paper sack and pulled the tab on a beer, pouring it into the yellow saucer that once served as an ashtray. "Don't worry, darling boo," she cooed to the cat. "We're gonna fix you right up. You'll be good as new in no time."

My Dad watched the entire bartending scene with interest and concern. This act of partaking of alcohol while in a vehicle came long before the Open Container law, so in a way, it was legal for a cat to booze it up while someone else was driving.

Even before Sandy could lower the saucer, the cat was standing on her hind legs, ready to get at the beer as if it were a lively mouse.

"Lord," Daddy said. "That's a shame, isn't it?"

Samantha slurped as if she hadn't had fluids in a week. She didn't pause until the saucer was dry. "Those PETA people find out about this and they'll come after you," he warned my sister, who was petting Sam and telling her, "Your nerves should be fine now, sweet baby kitty love. It's OK, Sammy Pooh."

"What happened to her fur?" Daddy asked. "What happened to her left ear? It's torn in half."

Sandy tipped the can of Bud Lite and refilled the cat's

saucer. "Fighting. She fights like a gator but not when she's buzzing. When she gets a good buzz, she's so gentle. See? Look at this baby love!"

Daddy drove along the interstate and every now and then would toss the cat his peripheral vision. He'd never seen such a mess and was wondering what our mother was going to do when he brought home this wreck of a drunken animal. The thing didn't want to stop drinking and continued until every bit of beer had been drained from the second round.

"Don't give that cat another drop," he ordered my sister. "I'm not going to be responsible for you killing it before we get home."

Sandy picked up Sam, who was now limp and purring, and held her up for Dad's inspection.

"Geez, this ain't right," Daddy said. He's college educated, but like many Southerners upon viewing something abnormal and shocking, will revert to the vernacular. "I ain't supporting this habit every day. We gotta get her on the Friskees and milk meal plan."

"You'll regret it if you don't aid and abet," Sandy said. "She's very mean and unpredictable if she doesn't get beer. Or wine. You can give her some of your jug wine, and she'll be fine with that. She's not particular and doesn't even need a cork."

"Funny. You're some kind of funny. Wait until your mama gets a load of that sot."

By the time they got home, the cat had awakened from the gauzy sleep of booze. She was not happy, but feisty and growling, trying to scratch my father and sister and arching her back with pure meanness.

"We better tank her up before your mama sees her," Dad said, becoming complicit in the act of bathing a cat in adult beverages. They gave Sam a snoot-full and went inside.

My mother, being devout in her faith and service work unto the Lord, accepted the cat and her flaws and was happy my father once again had someone to drink with come five o'clock every day. It was better than him heading somewhere like Bubba's Nudie Den.

Every evening, Daddy and Samantha would grab a couple of beers or a jug of wine and climb the stepladder to the roof of the house, where they could watch the sun slip into the white pines, oaks, and maples while they sipped and lapped up their spirits.

One day during their Happy Hour, the phone rang.

Mama picked it up. This was the sixth time the cemetery sales team had called our house in the past week, all of it starting with the release of the new church directory. Telemarketers like to snag those things, along with the obit and wedding pages of the paper.

"Do what?" Mama said. "Didn't I tell y'all I wasn't interested?"

The man on the other end was far too persistent and pesky, saying, "It's two-for-one, and we'll never have another special like this. It's now or never."

"You deserve this after the fine life you've led," the slick cemetery salesman said. "Consider yourself 'above' being in-the-ground types."

Mama was at the stove, her nightly perch, and wanting to get rid of him. "Well, you know…if you call back in an hour, my cat and my husband will be lit up enough he—my husband, not the cat—might just buy something from you."

After Daddy finally quit protesting and called the cemetery people, Mama phoned that night while I was coating pork chops in Shake'n Bake.

"Guess what we bought? You won't believe what your sweet daddy got us."

"Mmm. A condo at the beach."

"Oh, sugah. It's even better than that. It has heat and air, bathroom facilities, nice carpeting, and even a chapel."

"A Jesus RV?"

"That's sacrilegious."

"What then?"

"Guess."

"I can't. I'm worn out and my pork chops aren't doing well."

"Your precious daddy bought us two slots in a beautiful mausoleum nicer than any hotel we've ever stayed in. I just can't wait, Susan."

"Oh my Gawd."

"Say, 'Gosh.' Say, 'Oh my Gosh.' It's more Christian."

I was in shock and could say nothing.

"I owe it all to that poor, drunk cat. If it hadn't been for Samantha, I'd be buried in the ground just like everybody else. Can you believe it? A mausoleum?"

"That's wonderful."

"You know what the best part is?" she asked, in a state of euphoria.

"You get a free Bible?"

"Shush up. No. I put it all on VISA, and we got Frequent Flyer Miles and are using them for a trip to Spain."

"You're going to Spain with money earned from your funeral plots?"

"Of course," she said, and that's when she asked me "Will you keep Samantha while we're gone?"

"Well, now...I...well...I love the cat but—"

"You know she'll be fine as long as you don't forget Happy Hour."

"Right. Maybe I'll show her some of our grocery stores' finer wines."

*

P.S. Samantha lived 18 pickled years and died sober.

P.P.S. My parents visit their mausoleum slots once a week, still in awe.

Afternoon with a Buck

Roy Blount Jr.

This is a true story. That's the trouble with it. Not that it's true, but that I feel the need to tell people it is. Three days after these events happened to me—three days, that is, after I became the first person I have ever heard of who wrestled, physically, with an apparently lust-driven deer—I visited a movie set, where I told the story to everyone who would listen. Everyone looked professionally dubious. A prominent screenwriter was on hand to help punch up this movie's script from day to day, make it track better, give the characters clearer motivation. Two-thirds of the way through my story, the screenwriter frowned.

"Where would he get a brick?" he said.

"Not *he*," I said, "*me*. This happened to me. I just reached down, and there was a brick there, on the ground."

"What would a brick be doing there?" he wanted to know.

"I don't know," I said. "This *happened*. See, here are the scars."

I shouldn't have said that then, because—well, for one thing because it was too dramatic a thing to say on a movie set, since I wasn't in the movie. But also because it wasn't time in my story yet for the scars—I hadn't established how a person would get such scars from wrestling with a deer. Which is something that no one I have told this story to has ever heard of happening. It is a great story, in that sense.

Actually they weren't scars yet, they were cuts. But they looked as though they might become scars, if I kept picking at them. (Today, I regret to say, they are almost gone.) The scriptwriter wasn't motivated to do more than glance at them. I pushed on through to the end of the story. Except that I didn't have a good ending for it yet. I'm not sure that I have one now, but I do have an aftermath, which I lacked then.

"I thought you were going to do more with the red-sequin thing," the screenwriter said. "If not the pants."

If this were not a true story, I dare say I would do more with the red-sequin thing, because it was certainly a crucial element: Jessie Betts's skating dress. If not the pants.

Some backstory (I believe they call it in the movie industry): I divide my time between New York City and the country, western Massachusetts. So do my close friends, the Betts family. But they weren't coming up to the country on the weekend of September 22-23, 1990, because Jessie, their twelve-year-old daughter, had a big ice-skating competition in the city on the afternoon of Sunday the twenty-third. If she finished in the top three, she would go on to a higher-level competition at Lake Placid. And Jessie had left her red-sequin skating dress in their country house. So her mother, Lois, asked me whether I could possibly bring it in to the city in time for the competition.

I was more than happy. Here is something that I don't go into, usually, when I tell this story to people, but something that is true: I have always felt vaguely at fault with regard to women's clothes. I don't buy the right ones as presents, I don't compliment women on them sufficiently, I don't even notice them often enough, except to the extent that I find them provocative.

That is just the truth. And if it causes the woman reader of this story to turn against me as a narrator—as I say, I have always felt at fault with regard to women's clothes. And here was a chance to do a perfectly wholesome, positive, supportive, non-ulterior, clothes-affirming favor for a fine young woman of whom I am avuncularly fond.

I went to the Bettses' house and picked up Jessie's dress before noon. That gave me time to play tennis with my friend Jon Swan on the Bettses' court, which lies in a clearing in the woods behind their house.

I have a good first serve, when I get it in, but otherwise my tennis game is not, I like to believe, a reflection of my character. Jon is a decade or so older than I am and has a bad leg and a worse racket, but his play is clever, steady and amicably intent, whereas my ground-strokes fluctuate back and forth from overhit to tentative, my concentration is feverish one moment and miles away the next, I am often preoccupied with trying to think of some way to dissociate myself from my last shot (if not from my character) as I hit the next, and I lack (on those rare occasions when it might become an issue) a killer instinct.

In my day I have pressed strong opponents, however, and as someone who used to make a living as an interviewer I like to believe that when I hit a stretch of semiconsistent competence I at least draw something interesting out of more natural players, perhaps by dint of what Keats called (not in a tennis context) negative capability. Over the years I have mellowed to the point that I no longer scream and throw my racket.

And this was the first set I had played since the previous summer, so when I lost to Jon six-love without having got loose yet, and noticed that it was time to head toward the city, I was philosophical. After all, I was about to spend the rest of my afternoon coming to the aid of a promising young American figure skater.

Knowing the importance of my mission, Jon volunteered to sweep the court. I hustled up the path and emerged from the woods into the Bettses' backyard.

Where a deer stood.

Just stood there. About halfway between me and the Bettses' driveway, where my car was parked.

Deer abound in western Massachusetts. Once after a heavy rain I looked out the window of my own house and saw a big deer rushing downstream in the river. I thought maybe it was being swept away by the swollen current, but when I ran out and hollered "*Hey,*" the deer hooked a quick U-turn, swam back upstream a few yards and then jumped out of the water and ran through the middle of the village into the trees behind the general store.

That's what you expect a deer to do—flash into view and then modulate soundlessly off on tiny hard feet.

Or people kill them. One night on the road a big doe leapt out of the darkness and my right front fender hit her a glancing *whap*. I backed up and there she was in the middle of the road, on her knees and haunches, too stunned to be shooed out of harm's way. I ran to the nearest house, whose owner said, "Must've been thirty grazing out back the house at fresh dark," and called the state police. When we went back to check on her she was gone, and then we heard a *whump* and *crunch* up the road. A woman driving a pickup full of rocks had done for her, or another deer just like her, this time.

"*Awww*, I *hit* my brakes," the woman told us. "You'd miss 'em if they stopped, but they stop-and-start—aww, jumped right into me, well, here if you get the front feet and you get the back feet and just swing 'er up"—and she drove away with venison on the rocks.

The deer of my story, as I say, was just standing there. In the Bettses' backyard. I glanced at my watch, saw that I had a little leeway timewise, and thought to myself, "I believe I'll see how close I can get to this deer."

I crept toward him. He didn't move. I crept closer. He didn't move. He almost looked like he was looking at me, but I couldn't tell for sure. To the extent I could actually see his eye, it looked as if it might have a faraway look in it. It was black.

I crept closer, then I relaxed, stood up straight, walked right toward him. He didn't move.

At this point in the story people suspect a trick. "Stuffed, right?" some say. "You're going to tell me this was a stuffed deer." My agent, Esther Newberg, to whom I told this story the day after it happened—at that point I was still so stirred by the story that I thought her first reaction was going to be an eagerness to sell the movie rights. But no, what she said was, "Right, right, the Woody Allen moose, right? Wakes up on the bumper of the car."

And my own sister, Susan, said: "Is this going to be like the time in New Mexico we took that old dried-up deer carcass that the dogs drug up and we put it in your bed to see what you'd say when you pulled the covers back?" (Which is something my own sister actually did to me, years ago, when we were younger and more sportive.)

But no. This deer was not stuffed, nor temporarily stunned, nor dead. He actually shifted his stance a bit, but not much. I was only six feet away from him. I thought to myself, "I believe I am going to be able to *touch* this deer."

Which is something I've always wanted to do. To make physical contact with an independent wild animal. I guess everybody has a certain desire to do that, if it can be done safely. And a *deer!* A deer doesn't snarl, isn't off-putting, yet is almost the essence of wildness as in *there-it-is-vwoop-there-it-goes*.

I took two steps and put my hand between his horns.

He didn't mind. Not very soft to the touch: ridged coarse hair on hard skull, like a cow's head.

I scratched. He seemed to *like* it. In fact, he butted forward slightly, as if appreciatively, moving into my stroke as a cat will. But unlike a cat's, this deer's head wasn't very pettable from my point of view. As opposed to his, evidently.

I thought: This is neat. Then I thought: This is weird.

Childish thoughts. But linking up with a wild animal is something I have been thinking about since childhood, when stories led me to identify with so many rabbits and bears. (And how about *Bambi?* I came to the end of that book and I said to myself, "Wait a minute. The *mother dies?* I'm a little kid! Why would they give me a book where the mother dies? Are they trying to tell me something? My mother looks healthy . . . ." And in *The Yearling,* the boy had to shoot his pet deer. Damn.)

And then I thought: These *horns* I'm scratching between. They're horns. Altogether four points. It seemed to me that I had probably been scratching this deer's head long enough. I couldn't see that it was leading anywhere. "Okay, then," I said briskly (the only time either the deer or I spoke.) I made to take my leave.

The deer wouldn't let me. That is to say, as soon as I took my hand away he took a step forward, pushing his head into my midsection. I grabbed his horns, close to his head. He took another step.

I didn't want to back up. It wasn't a big issue with me, I didn't feel that I had anything to prove, exactly, to this deer or to myself. But everything considered I didn't like the idea of backing down. The deer pressed forward.

I was wondering, why is this deer doing this? It didn't

accord with any deer behavior I had ever observed or heard about. He was so intent on it. As though it was just something that he'd always wanted to do. He of course had no responsibilities, it meant nothing to him that Jessie needed her red-sequin dress.

Then I noticed he was drooling.

Could you get rabies from a deer? But he wasn't showing any interest in biting me. I had never in fact heard of deerbite. You could get Lyme disease from a deer tick, I knew, but I had never heard of anyone getting deer ticks directly from a deer.

At any rate, there we were. I felt strong enough to hold him at . . . well, "at bay" didn't seem to be the expression. To a standstill. But for how long?

Enough. I had things to do. I gave the deer a brisk shove, freed my hands and flapped my pants at him.

I was wearing shorts. From the tennis. I had my long pants tucked under my arm. Waving my pants at him required that I push off and do a quick snatch-and-wave, and I didn't get a very good grip on my pants, and my tennis racket—which was also tucked under my arm—slipped down between my elbow and my hip, and what with one thing and another, my pants wound up on the ground. The deer, recoiling slightly, glanced down at them.

I didn't feel secure about bending down to pick them up. The deer butted at them tentatively. Then he lifted his head. My pants were hooked on one of his horns.

Oh, Lord, I thought. This deer is going to run off into the forest with my pants. Containing my wallet. And my car keys.

Which means, how can I get Jessie's red-sequin skating dress to her in time for her competition?

I grabbed my racket and hit at my pants. They came loose. I didn't feel secure about bending down to pick them up, though. The deer surged forward. I grabbed his horns again, in the process dropping my racket.

And there we were. I was reminded of the story of an Irish soldier who, in a battle against the Turks, cried out to a comrade, "I've caught a Tartar!"

"Bring him along then," said the comrade.

"He won't come."

"Then, come along yourself."

"Arrah, but he won't let me."

If you are attacked by a shark or a bear, I had heard, your best bet is to punch it in the nose. But it is hard to get a blow to the head in when you're in a clinch. I did manage to frap the deer's nose with my knuckles. It felt like—well, you don't get any gratification from hitting a deer in the nose. And the deer didn't seem to mind it. I twisted his head one way, and then the other. He seemed actually to relish this.

I decided to bulldog him down. I pushed his head all the way to the ground—lowering myself, in the process, to one knee. I didn't get him turned over, though, the way rodeo guys do a steer. His head was on the ground, but the rest of him was under no pressure to follow it. All four of his feet remained planted. And what if I did get him tumped over—those sharp toes thrashing around... Then I noticed that his points were now very close to my groin. I stood up again, and his head came with me. And there we were.

This was not like anything I had experienced before. I guess you could say the same about anything you haven't experienced before. But this was like—well it wasn't like having a coat rack come alive in your hands, and it wasn't like getting entangled with a stranger's umbrella while trying to get off the subway, and it wasn't like being proffered a lion's foot and seeing a thorn in it. Maybe it was something like quitting smoking; but I never have smoked.

Either I was tiring, or he was pushing harder. I gave some ground. I had the feeling that the deer, if he wanted to, could push harder still. And he had more traction than I did, and his horns were harder than my hands—I wasn't holding the points, but the parts I was holding were rough, almost like coral, and what if he got a temper up . . .

"Were you scared?" I was asked by people to whom I told this story early on.

"Yes," I answered, until my friend Vereen Bell said, "That's hard to imagine, being scared of a deer."

"Not so much *scared*," I have told people since. "I mean, I knew he wasn't going to kill me. But what if he got frightened and started slashing around? Deer use their horns to fight off wolves, right? I could imagine getting gouged enough that I'd have to go to the emergency room. You don't mess around with a wild-animal puncture. And then how would I get to New York in time with Jessie's red-sequin skating dress?

I was scared. I was backing up bit by bit to keep my arms

extended; every bit of extension I lost, the deer took it up like slack.

I *could* have called out to Jon, who was down in the woods sweeping the court. But I didn't want to. Maybe if he hadn't just beaten me six-love I would have, but I don't think so. I felt this was something I ought to be able to deal with myself. Anyway, what would I have called out, exactly?

"Jon! Could you come up here quick? I . . . I'm . . . I've got ahold of a deer and he won't let me turn him loose!"?

No. Jon is a writer too, and this was my story. I tried to put myself in the deer's place. What did deer do with their horns, usually? Besides fight wolves. Bump and rub them off on trees. Did this deer think I was a tree? Maybe he was wondering why this tree was behaving like this.

I decided to shift him off onto a real tree. He might be relieved. I backed around in the yard, looking over my shoulder for trees, finding a couple of little ones. What did he need with them, he had me.

I backed further, into some bushes. This felt like a bad move. I minded being in these bushes more than the deer seemed to. And now I didn't have anywhere further to back. I looked down.

That's when I saw the brick.

Several women I have told this story to have had a real problem with the brick. Not on narrative grounds, but because they disapprove of violence to deer. So do I, I assure them. But Jessie was waiting . . .

If this were fiction maybe I would have the red-sequin

dress under my arm. Maybe the dress would be what attracted the deer. Maybe the deer would knock me down and make me wear it. But no. The dress was waiting in the car.

And the brick came to hand. People have bricks in their yards, right?

I turned loose with my right hand long enough to pick up the brick and bonk the deer on the nose with it. The deer seemed startled, in a tentative way. The brick didn't feel good in my hand, but I hit him harder with it—not *hard* hard, but hard enough that he pulled back, somewhat.

He looked at me, noncommittally. I was tired of this! I needed space! I wanted my pants! I wanted to get rid of the brick, get rid of the deer. I threw the brick at him. That did the trick, he sprang away.

"Jon!" I yelled. "Come up here! The strangest thing!"

I saw that my right hand was bleeding. I ran to the Bettses' swimming pool and stuck it in.

Jon witnessed the deer, standing a few yards away looking enigmatic, and he also saw my wounds. You could write him care of the *Columbia Journalism Review,* where he is an editor. Would I make that up? I'm an old journalist myself. Jon also recalls that I was flushed and breathing hard, which I suppose is true enough but I feel he puts too much emphasis on it. Of course he didn't see any of the actual wrestling itself.

I went to the Swans' house and Marianne Swan bandaged the cuts and I drove to the city holding my hand above my heart—all the way, for two hours, so it wouldn't bleed anymore (Marianne's idea). I got the dress to Jessie in time.

And the rest of this story is telling it to people, most of which I have already told you about. The Bettses said the deer must have been the same one they'd seen lurking around in their yard the previous weekend. Their bulldog, Max, an amiable and forthright animal, had run him off twice. (Once when the Betts were at my house I carelessly shoved an armload of wastepaper into the fireplace, the fire blazed out into the living room, and Max jumped up and *attacked the fire.* It backed down.) The Bettses had been told that the deer was probably one of several that another family in the area had been feeding all summer. So he'd lost his fear of people.

My friend Jim Seay, a deer hunter, put in that it was rutting season. At that time of year hunters sometimes clack two old racks of antlers together and male deer come running, looking to butt heads. "Your deer was horny," Jim said. "I never knew heard of one hooking up with a person like that, though." I thought he might sound more envious, somehow. He sounded...sympathetic.

Here is my son Kirven's response to the story: "I'd probably have done the same thing myself." A generous thing for a son to tell a father. I feel bad that I didn't think to tell him in return, "I'd probably have done, myself, all the things I've given you a hard time about." I might say that there seemed to be a note of *resignation* in his voice. When something happens to your father you can't help thinking, deep inside, "Ah. Yes. This is the kind of thing the men of my family do."

Actually Kirven might well have handled the deer better than I did. He can beat me in tennis, and he has always had a way with animals. When he was little he told his mother, "I go up to dogs I don't even know and whisper, 'I love you.'"

Maybe I should have whispered something to the deer, or chanted something, or jumped on his back and ridden him off into the woods. This story could use a transcendent moment. But I had to get away, there was Jessie's dress. Which, as I say, I got to her on time. She skated with aplomb. She missed, by one point, making the top three and Lake Placid, but that didn't get her down.

A couple of weeks later, the deer approached a man who was doing some work on the Bettses' house. The man called the game warden, who shot the deer with a tranquilizer dart and took his horns off with a chainsaw. Nobody has reported seeing the deer since. Maybe he was cured of being a people animal, or maybe he let a hunter get close to him during deer week this winter and died wondering what he may also have wondered when he and I parted: Hey, what is the *story* here? But that is just speculation on my part.

*

Fade out, freeze frame, whatever works. How often does a true story end satisfactorily? In the end you throw a brick at it.

FROM BOY WITH LOADED GUN

LEWIS NORDAN

One weekend as Dorris and Helga and I were sitting together at the Laundromat, something happened that sparked a change in my living circumstances. Dorris and Helga were big readers, and so, as we always did, we were all sitting there in the Highland Park Laundromat reading novels, side by side. The machines were going, the chairs were pretty uncomfortable, but in fact I was feeling happy in the company of my new friends. I was reading *A Fan's Notes* and considering my next gratitude list. I was grateful I wasn't as bad off as the poor drunk in the book, that was something to be grateful for, and I was also thinking I would include Dorris and Helga in my next list. I was truly grateful for the time we spent together. The fact that they were literary people was a part of what appealed to me, though their tastes were old-fashioned and frankly a little odd. Dorris read Tolstoy almost exclusively—"The sweep, the panorama!" he would suddenly exclaim, "the fragile single hearts!"—and Helga always had clutched in her huge prison-guard hands some delicate volume of poetry, Rilke or Lord knows what else. Sometimes she would look up from her reading and her face would be beatific, it's the only word that really describes her. She might read a line or two aloud to the two of us, something about the springtime greenness of the trees coming into leaf being a form of grief, and her voice would catch, her eyes would become moist, and then she would fall silent again, and look again deep into her book as if into deep clear water. Such comfortable, sweet moments occurred to the accompaniment of the coin changer as it dispensed silver in casinolike bursts of generosity, and to the easy evensong of the dryers, the abrupt gush of water in the Fill cycle, the dogged and determined chuffing of Wash, or the reckless centrifugal abandon of Spin.

One day in the midst of this music, the elfin Dorris and his strapping wife asked whether I would like to share supper with them that night in their home. This was the first time either had suggested broadening the range of our relationship, and it came to me like an incredible gift. A home, a real home, like the one I had lost.

"Yes," I said, "oh yes, yes, yes, thank you, yes." Later, after a fragrant lamb stew that Helga had prepared in their little kitchen, with its red-checkered café curtains, the three of us sat in their den and took off our shoes and put up our feet and chatted quietly until we were all talked out, sleepy and scarcely able to move from our chairs with a drowsy pleasant lethargy.

Dorris and Helga sat together on an ancient leather sofa and I took the matching easy chair.

Their next offer was an answered prayer. They invited me to move out of the YMCA and into their spare room. The room had no furniture, they warned, not even a bed, and I would be obliged to sleep on the floor, but without a moment's hesitation I said yes, again, yes, yes, oh God yes, thank you, yes.

Need I bother to say that I overlooked many signals that might have clued me that this would turn out to be a bad idea? The most obvious of these was that to prepare the stew Helga had worn a sort of costume. While Dorris and I sat in the den and chatted, Helga busied herself in the kitchen and indeed cooked the entire meal while wearing stiletto heels and the frilly apron, and the fishnet stockings and the dustcap of a French maid in a farce. This was all she wore while she cooked. The daintiness of the costume emphasized the manly height and bulk of her stature. I had seen this, taken mental note of the lunatic oddity of it, and yet the instant the offer came, I agreed to move in to their spare room.

It did not occur to me to use this information to help me make a decision about staying the night, or indeed moving in with this strange couple. There being no bed for me did not even register with me as an unusual detail. I can't explain this satisfactorily except to say that in a sense Helga was always in costume, her clothing never suited her enormous physical presence in any space she occupied. The French maid costume was certainly her most extravagant offering, but not essentially different from her many other fashion choices. I had overlooked much already; this was merely one more thing.

Or maybe the only explanation that anyone needs is that anything on earth would have seemed more normal than an army cot at the Y. Even an attitude of gratitude could not cancel the YMCA barracks and what it told me about how far I had fallen. I would have overlooked anything to escape my current reality, the "life on life's terms." Dorris and Helga, eccentric though they might have been, were the lemons life was dealing me to make lemonade.

That really must have been what I told myself, if I told myself anything at all. Or maybe—this of course is in terrible hindsight—I was preparing for that most abnormal state of all, which I was soon to enter, to be a parent at the graveside of his child. That, however, is another story, one that I have already told as well as I know how.

Helga provided me with a pillow and a blanket, and so there on the hardwood floor for the first time I rested my grateful bones and soon I was asleep. No mattress had ever seemed so comfortable as that solid slab of wood. I scarcely turned over during the night. I woke rested and well. Dorris and Helga were still asleep behind the closed door of their bedroom. I folded my blanket and put it with my pillow in a corner of the room. I dressed and left the house and made my way downtown to the Y, where I unloaded my locker into a duffel bag and stood at the corner near Market Square and grabbed a PAT bus and moved fully into my new digs. I had a new home, a real home in a real house.

I saw little of Dorris and Helga during the day, it turned out. For various reasons, some of my own doing, we saw each other only slightly more often than before I moved in. For one thing, I didn't want to become a Ramon-style boarder. Mornings they came from their room, but they said little and only moved slowly about the house. I followed their lead and was a silent shadow in their midst. There was a crude, cold-water shower and toilet and a big shard of mirror in the cellar where I made my morning ablutions, and this was fine with me. We began to coexist. I felt very free to take my turn in the real bathroom of this house, but I preferred cold water and privacy for now to almost any other comforts of home. This new arrangement was so far superior to my recent communal showers at the Y as to leave me giddy with gratitude.

My usual routine was to rise early and to walk to a regular early meeting in a church basement nearby. First Things First was the name of the 7 A.M. meeting that I liked. The same people usually showed up, only a few early risers, so it was an especially comfortable place to have my morning coffee. Dorris and Helga were usually still asleep when I left the house. After the meeting I went with a few other guys, "recovering alcoholics," as we called ourselves, to Ritter's Diner for eggs. Wednesday mornings there was a meeting right there in the diner, in a back room, where the diner supplied the coffee and you could order breakfast. This section of Pittsburgh is full of shady streets and flowering gardens and small home-owned businesses and friendly faces. It was within walking distance of my new home. By the time I had finished breakfast, the day had begun to heat up and I had said good-bye to my breakfast companions and was sitting in my nicely ventilated room at Dorris and Helga's place, cross-legged on the floor in front of my Smith-Corona with a sheet of paper rolled in, and life was good.

Oh life was very good. I had my own key, so I came and went freely. Dorris and Helga were out, usually, by this time. They both had jobs. What could have been more fine? I made a point of taking all my meals outside the house, so as not to impose upon my hosts' hospitality, and this arrangement worked very well. Evenings when Helga and Dorris were home, together the three of us sat and watched the evening news and chatted quietly, and then usually we turned off the TV and sat and read in silence until bedtime. Helga's costumes were never so extreme again as when she prepared dinner that first night, but usually she did seem more or less outlandishly attired. She had an outfit I thought of as her milkmaid costume, with a bonnet and apron and wooden pail, and another I am not sure how to characterize but possibly Mennonite, or maybe only a country librarian. It was hard to say. I was shy to question her about this game of dress-up that she seemed always to be playing, though I often complimented the way she looked, and always she thanked me. Once or twice she said something like, "I hope this doesn't just seem silly to you" or "You don't think this one goes a little too far, do you," and always I would assure her, "No, absolutely not, not at all."

After I had lived in this home thus serenely for perhaps three weeks, Dorris took me aside one day and showed me an expensive toy of sorts that apparently he had owned for some time. This was the first time their eccentricity took on what might have been an unhealthy, or possibly dangerous, quality. Helga was not in the house when this initial conversation occurred, as Dorris had made certain, for this little talk, Dorris's body language seemed to say, was just between us men. He invited me into his and Helga's bedroom, where at the foot of their big bed stood an old-fashioned steamer trunk, with wooden bands and leather straps and a big brass lock. He closed the bedroom door discreetly behind us and went immediately to the trunk, which he unlocked, a little mysteriously I have to say.

"Helga has a key, too, of course," he assured me, unnecessarily.

Out of the trunk he lifted, when the great lid was open, what seemed to be a dark metal box about three feet square. Extending from the box, attached to it somehow, octopuslike, were several dangling flexible "arms," flopping this way and that, chaotically, as he transferred the box from the steamer trunk to the made-up bed, where he placed it on the quilt that covered the bed. The box reminded me strongly of the robot on the old *Lost in Space* TV show, the one that was forever flopping its arms about and saying, "Danger, Will Robinson. Danger!" In fact, from somewhere deep inside me I thought I heard a similar warning, equally urgent, "Danger, Buddy Nordan. Danger!" There was also, I noticed, a cord and plug dangling down, so that the box could be plugged into an electrical socket in the wall. This was some kind of machine, I was beginning to realize.

"I don't show many people this baby," Dorris confided to me.

I could think of nothing to say, nothing at all. I spent my days talking to people who were trying to make sense of their alcohol-shattered lives. In meetings and over coffee we spoke of God's grace and of service to others and making amends for the wreckage of our past. We "worked steps" that we believed, on faith and on observation of others like us, would lead not merely to a sober life but to spiritual awakenings in our drug-deadened selves. In my most peaceful hours I breathed the damp air of church basements. I visited Veterans Administration hospitals and prisons and halfway houses and rehabs and detox units in hopes of offering comfort to someone like myself and thereby acquiring one more day's sobriety for myself. I ate doughnuts and drank coffee and prayed on my knees to stay sober one day at a time. None of what I did during a day prepared me for this moment. Indeed, in my solitary hours I wrote stories about a boy who longs for his alcoholic father's love in Mississippi. I identified as much with the father as the son. Weekends I stood in a phone booth on a corner and talked to my own sons, whose hearts I feared I had broken. What did I know of black boxes drawn from a steamer trunk? What, in fact, was I doing in Pittsburgh, where I was less than merely a new person, I was an alien being?

 I looked at the box on the bed. The flexible arms of the mechanical octopus—the robot, whatever it was—were fitted with one of two types of devices at the end. One was a funnel-shaped affair, and the other was a smaller connecting attachment. I could make no sense of any of it. Dorris plugged the box into the wall socket and left it on the bed and went back to the steamer trunk. He bent down and this time he pulled out of the trunk, like a rabbit from a magician's hat, a large, flat, black leather case of a certain kind, a sort of portfolio-like affair, that he laid out on the bed and then flung open with a flourish.

I'd seen a couple of movies and TV shows in which big-city black-market gunrunners displayed their samples of handguns in much the same way, in a similar case. When the leather case was open fully, it could be seen to be fitted on the inside with clear plastic pockets, just like the cases the black-marketeers used to display their wares, but whatever it was I was looking at in these pockets, they were not firearms. I couldn't tell what they were, at the time. My eyes took in the images but my mind would not translate what I saw.

There were nine clear plastic pockets, three across, three up and three down. Each pocket held a single solid brick-red colored cylinder of some kind, each exactly alike except in size. Each cylinder, from left to right, grew progressively diminished in size. The first cylinder in the first pocket was a foot long, approximately, and nine or ten inches in diameter. The others were smaller, down to the ninth pocket, which held a cylinder only two or three inches long and thin as a pencil. Dorris removed the first of these, the largest, from its pocket and showed it to me.

Realization came to me with dizzying force. Perfectly and realistically shaped artifical penises in nine sizes, brick-red in color, as I said. Big red cocks, nine of them, on display, count them for yourself.

Dorris unsnapped the first pocket in the case, as I said, and brought out the largest dildo and held it in his open palm. He proffered it to me. I stood with my hands at my side, unable to move just yet. He squeezed it and opened his palm again. He kept holding it out, in my direction.

"Take a look at this baby," he said, extending it to me. "Go ahead, take it, give it a squeeze."

As if I were a robot myself instead of a man who prayed each morning and each night and spoke of a Power Greater Than Myself and believed, however clumsily, that God's grace had taken away my self-destructive compulsion to drink alcohol, I took the foot-long cock into my own hand, I held it, I tested its heft and bulk, I gave it a squeeze. I offer no explanation or apology. The dildo was made of high quality hard red rubber. It was firm and well-veined and the head was large and well-shaped with a small opening in the tip. I looked at the big cock there in my hand. I squeezed it again.

I said, "Yeah, that's something, all right."

Dorris took the rubber cock from me and confidently attached it to the end of one of the octopus arms fitted with a connecting device, not a funnel. It snapped securely into place. He held it up briefly for me to see, as much as to say "Voila." He reached then for a switch on the fucking machine—for this is the name I learned to call it by, this black box—and clicked it into the On position, and immediately a sound issued from the box that was both unnerving and self-explanatory. I knew it for what it was, I knew this gasp and grunt to be the sound of an air compressor, plain and simple. Inside the black box a motor was operating a small compressor and pump that, in turn, operated the octopus arms of the machine, and therefore the dildo attachment. The sound that it made was at once a sigh and a groan, slow and as filled with sexual resignation and guilty desire as a sound from human lungs and throat.

Dorris said, "I like to think of it as the Amazing Technicolor Fucking Machine." I managed not even a smile at this joke, though some sort of sound did issue from my mouth, something low and indescribable. Now when he handed the foot-long rubber cock back to me I had to hold on tight, for compressed air pumping thought the flexible arm in short bursts caused the dildo to take life. The machine gasped and sighed, the cock in my hand squirmed and pulsed, it took up a regular stroking motion, and I had to hold it tight in my hand to keep it from jumping away from me.

Dorris may have noticed my discomfort, for he took the dildo from me and tossed it lightly onto the quilt on the bed, where the huge red cock pulsed and squirmed and stroked empty air, seeming almost to crawl across the covers of the bed in search of something.

We said nothing, either of us, for what seemed to me a very long time. We only stood and watched the dildo, and listened to the disturbing sounds of the machine that drove it.

At last he did speak. He said, "Some day, when you feel comfortable of course, not a minute before, I hope you'll slip one of these cocks into Helga. She'd like that very much, you know."

I couldn't speak. I could only stand and watch the slow strokes of the dildo across the covers of the bed. By my silence I must have seemed to give my assent. Dorris went on talking about the machine. He told me everything.

"If you're at all interested..." he said.

Still I could not speak and so he deftly dropped the subject.

He and Helga had taken the fucking machine to a Swingers Club meeting once, he told me, and one woman agreed to try it out, but "All in all, I'd have to say it didn't go over particularly well."

Flagged, Flim-Flammed, and Fingerprinted

M.L. Davis

My new teaching job required that I be fingerprinted. Having never been fingerprinted, I had mixed emotions about this. Knowing that I am not a criminal, I felt a bit insulted by the prospect, but knowing also that pedophiles can be present in schools these days, I gave in to the concept of the greater good.

I had to renew my driver's license before I could be fingerprinted because the sticker that shows the expiration date had fallen off the back of it. I had been told repeatedly to go to the courthouse in Hahnville, Louisiana, to renew my license since there was no line. No line sounded like a good thing in the heat of June in New Orleans, so I filled my tank with three-dollar-a-gallon gas and took my thirty-mile ride to Hahnville. Everyone was right: there was no line. Not only was there no line, but the people were friendly. Decidedly different from pre-Katrina experiences. The lady ahead of me was Miss Clotilde, whom everyone at the courthouse knew. Miss Clotilde was tired of worrying about storms, she told us, so she had bought herself a double-wide on four acres in Amite. Her house was for sale: three bedrooms, two baths, brick. I didn't ask Miss Clotilde why she felt the need to leave an undamaged brick house to move into a trailer, but that's how some people think since Katrina ravaged this part of the country. No logic, just gut reactions that start them chasing their tails. Miss Clotilde brought a check for her license. "Now, Miss Clotilde, didn't that son of yours tell you we only take cash? He's a deputy."

"Didn't tell me nothin', chere. I guess I got to drive home and come back. I'll see you in a little bit."

My turn. Fastest license stop ever. I breezed through the eye exam, presented my insurance and title, and we headed to the computer so I could pay my $18.50.

"Uh oh. You got a flag, honey," said the jovial secretary.

"What's a flag?" I asked.

"You have a car with no insurance."

"I've got one car, and you're holding the insurance paper in your hand."

"It says you have a 1996 Mercury that you cancelled this insurance on in 2006."

"I gave that car to my son in 2004, and we went together to have the title transferred, and he had it insured by State Farm."

"Did you go to Spasey & Spasey for the transfer?"

"Yes, we did," I said.

She laughed. "They're notorious for not filing the paperwork, honey. Here, call their office, and then call the DMV, and they'll tell you what to do. I'm sorry. You can come back here, or you can go the DMV, pay the fine, and they'll give you your license."

"Fine?" I asked.

"$225 for cancelled insurance."

"You're kidding. Because Spasey & Spasey didn't do their job, I have to pay a fine?"

"Happens all the time, honey."

I thanked the woman and left. So much for saving time, I thought. But seeing the bright side, I realized that it was good this happened now when I wasn't teaching and had time to deal with it. I would make the phone calls and clear up the mistake.

I called the title company an hour later when I got home and told them what had happened. There was silence on the other end of the line. "I'm sure we filed the paperwork. That was three years ago, before Katrina."

"Yes, so why didn't I receive the transfer papers?" I asked.

"Well, you said you paid $26.50 and $20.00…that means you were requesting a copy of your title because you lost the original."

"I didn't lose the original. I have a receipt for $86.50 that says 'transfer of title.' I'm looking at it. Those other fees are what you charged to do the transfer."

"Well, if you paid it, we filed it. You must have lost it. Maybe we mailed it and you threw it out in the junk mail."

"Why would I throw away a license plate? I go through all my mail before I throw anything away. That's an important document," I said calmly.

"Well, you know that was so long ago, and we've had Katrina. If you want to come in we'll do it again for you."

"Ma'am, do you understand that my son bought another car in 2006? We don't need to transfer the title now."

"Well, I can't help you," she said.

I called the DMV. I was told to gather my paperwork showing we had applied for the transfer, show my son's insurance paperwork proving that the car had been insured, and write a letter to the DMV explaining the situation. Present it at the DMV office. The lady said that should take care of the problem.

Now the DMV is quite an experience. An auditorium-sized room is filled with 200 chairs, all of which were occupied by criminal types like myself. I was told to put my name on the list and I'd be given a number. I searched for a seat, waited for someone's number to be called, and took the empty chair. I noticed that people were staring into space. Others were complaining to strangers around them about the time spent waiting. No one read. I opened my new Anita Shreve summer read and was well into *Resistance* when my number was called. I was 742, proceeding to table 15.

I explained the situation, and the lady was lovely. I noticed that all the state employees had a very quiet and helpful attitude. I think they had had post-K training in how not to rile the inmates of the area. Be nice to avoid mass shootings. Anyway, she told me my paperwork was in perfect order, and I really didn't need it anyway because they had all the information in the computer. It showed my son's name and his insurance company, and that he had cancelled the insurance in 2006 when he bought a new vehicle.

"So we can just get rid of this flag and get you your license," she said. "Now, I need your son's full name."

"Why do you need my son's name?" I asked.

"Well, we're moving the flag from your license and putting it on to his," she explained.

"Wait a minute," I said. "Why are you flagging my son's license?"

"Well, somebody has to pay the $225 fine, so we'll let him pay it when he renews his license."

"But you just told me the paperwork was in order."

She smiled patiently. "It is in order, but somebody has to pay the fine."

"So, explain what my son will have to do to get the flag off his license if I move it to him."

"Well," she began, "he'll have to call State Farm and get the car insured. Then you two will have to go back to Spasey & Spasey to do another title transfer. Then, when they send him the paperwork, he can pay the fine." She smiled.

I did the math in my head and realized my son would shell out $500 to get the flag off his license, not to mention the days off work it would take to get it all done...for a car that hadn't been driven since 2006. "I'll keep the flag," I announced.

"That would be the easier thing to do," she reassured me. "That will be $225 cash."

"Cash? I have to go get the cash. Do I have to get back in the line when I return?"

"Oh, no, ma'am. You just go to the desk, and he'll send you right here." She smiled again. They probably pray daily not to be shot by someone who just can't take anymore of this bullshit, I thought as I walked out to my car.

I became determined to finish this task before close of business. I was on day three of renewing my license, and I needed my fingerprints. Back in nearly an hour, I was whisked to table 15 only to find my lady gone to lunch. She had been replaced by a man with a heavy accent. Quick prayer: don't let me have to start this process over again. I told him I had gone to cash a check. No problem, he told me. He took my money. I smiled. He told me to follow him and he would get me out of there fast. I paid $18.50 to a cute young girl at the desk, and Elvira, the photographer, took my glamor shot—good for four years. I was on my way to the sheriff's office.

*

Never be in need of quick help at a police station. I walked into a lobby of sorts that was encased in Plexiglas. A sign read "Ring Bell." I rang. I waited. Not being one to tick off police, I decided one ring was enough. I was reading the wanted posters when the door swung open, and a woman raced in from the street. "I'm being stalked," she told me rather urgently. The last episode of *The Sopranos* flashed before me. I had survived the flim-flam and the flag, but I could get shot at the finger printer's.

"Is he following you?" I asked as I took a small step back. I rang the bell again.

"No, but I called the police yesterday and they came to my house and this morning I got up and he had climbed my back fence and left fresh flowers and balloons on my patio and I have a glass door there and he could have come in. What should I do?" She pulled off her sunglasses and stuck them into her bra that was showing from the plunging neckline of her tee shirt.

Does she think I'm the sheriff? I wondered. "I'd tell the police again," I said.

"Where are these people anyway?" she asked. She rang the bell and knocked on the window. Oh, great. The cop will be angry and screw up my fingerprints, and I'll be pegged for a rapist.

"And I have to get my son to work. Where are these people?!"

I seriously considered leaving quickly and letting the stalked one deal with the aggravated cop, but I was too late. The cop appeared. "Hi, y'all. How can I help you today?" Big smile. She had an accent like the actress Holly Hunter.

"I need fingerprints for my job, but she has a stalker and needs some advice."

"Who's stalking you, ma'am? Have you filed a police report? Can't let these people get away with that kind of stuff."

"I filed a report yesterday, but I need a restraining order. But I have to get my son to work. He can't be late. How long will it take?"

"A deputy can be here in fifteen minutes, ma'am," answered this deputy.

"Oh, maybe I should leave and come back later after I take my son to work."

"Well, ma'am," the deputy said, "it's 2:00. What time does your son have to be at work?"

"5:00," the bosomy blonde responded, "but, you know how kids are…he likes to have time to put his makeup on."

I kept a straight face and nodded. After all, this *is* New Orleans. He could be a mime, a clown. Oh, a transvestite in a bar, I was told.

"Why not sit down and wait, then take him to work. You have three hours," I said. "He'll understand." I wondered if I should have said "she'll."

She agreed and sat on a bench. The deputy called someone on the phone and then turned her attention to me.

"Driver's license and $10," she smiled. "What's your social?"

I told it to her, and she talked constantly to me as she typed the information off my license. I tried not to respond for fear she would make a mistake. One number off and I'm a criminal…handcuffed….ruined…Just type please, I thought.

"Follow me," she said, and she buzzed me through to her office. "Now stand right behind me in this exact spot." Another big smile from her. "Get real close to me. Now, I'm going to move, but you stand very still on this spot and do not look down, whatever you do. Give me your hand."

"Why can't I look down?" I asked.

"Don't talk right now," she of the incessant talking said. "I can tell you're a teacher."

I made no response. I was following orders.

"Teachers have ruined fingerprints from the chalk dust. I have to hope I get good ones. Chalk dries out your fingertips so bad that your prints start to fade."

"I don't use chalk," I dared to say.

"Doesn't matter. You used to. The damage is done."

I was doubting this was true. "Finished," she announced cheerfully. "You should be glad you came in today to do this because next week we're going to print people on the computer. I'm training on it this week, and it's so sensitive that I moved my hand on the screen by accident and it booked me as a criminal. Just that fast." She rushed on. "I had to call my boss, and he had a fit. He had to write to the FBI and Homeland Security, and he had to fax all my records to Washington to get me taken out of the criminal system. You sure can't make a mistake on *that* computer. Now, you take your prints to your new employer, and they'll send them to Baton Rouge. If they can't read them, you'll have to come in again, so keep your receipt and I won't charge you again. Put a lot of heavy cream on your fingertips at night, and it might help your prints get clearer." She patted me on the back after telling me a brief version of her life story, and at 2:40 I left her office.

The Stalked One was speaking to a deputy, and she was telling him she had to get her son to work. I wondered the rest of the day just how long it took him to put on his makeup for work. My work for the day was finished, and I was going to meet a friend for coffee. I checked my purse for money. After paying $386.50 for a set of fingerprints, I wanted to be sure I could afford a café au lait. Maybe I should have committed a crime. At least I could have been fingerprinted for free.

Judging the Sibling Summer Olympics

Lisa Earle McLeod

Ahhh, summer in the South. Budweisers, boating, and the chance to bond with your extended family. In my family, we have a long-standing tradition of spending a week together at my parents' lake house.

The merrymakers consist of myself, my two grown siblings (a brother and a sister), our spouses, our collective gaggle of kids aged two months to twelve years, and of course my parents, all packed into a thirty-year-old, three-bedroom, split-level lake house for a week of fun in the sun.

All I can say is, there's nothing like some quality time with Mom and Dad to shine the light on your dysfunctions.

After our most recent trip, I began to think my siblings were raised by wolves. After several years of living in other parts of the country, it appears that not only did they have the audacity to marry people different from us and breed with them; but they have also completely abandoned our own family's solid gold standards and are now deferring to the bizarre ways of their mates.

At first, I thought it might have been jet lag. Or perhaps my slacker sibs had forgotten to give their spouses the briefing on proper Earle family vacation etiquette. But no, after a few days at the lake it became evident that the imported spouses had no intention of shaping up and learning how to act like us.

Several of the imports were oblivious to the proper way to wash a dish. Hellooo? It's called a dishwasher for a reason—you don't need to scrape the crud off before you put the plates in. They also enforced weird rules like making their kids bathe after digging for goo in the lake, and one of them even thought people should use a fork when snagging a cube of watermelon from the communal bowl.

Who are these people?

To give you a bit of background, family custom dictates that the Earles spend the better part of our vacation trying to outdo one another on the water-ski course. Being a somewhat competitive brood, my siblings and I dedicated our childhoods to trying to best each other at just about everything, and water-skiing has always been one of our favorite venues.

However, as we've aged and become less limber than we used to be, the competition to see who can make the most buoys on the slalom water course has cooled, and we've moved on to the real event of the Sibling Summer Olympics: a subtle and insidious game called "Who runs a better life?"

It's where each family attempts to prove that they are in fact at the top of the sibling heap. The events range from "proper towel-folding technique" and "spouse management skills" to "appropriate toddler nutrition" and the "most exhaustive political argument."

Yet despite the daily elimination rounds, it became painfully apparent that some of these clueless spouses didn't even realize they were being judged. Do they actually think we come on vacation to have fun?

Perhaps all the drinking lulled them into thinking this was supposed to be leisure time. I guess they didn't realize that alcohol is not the game itself; it's part of the equipment, kind of like a Power-Aid we use to sustain ourselves through the rigors of competition. (It can also help drown the agony of defeat, but more about that later.)

I was OK at first when the outsider spouses chose to sit on the sidelines during the "Who has the coolest job?" race. (Being the oldest, I'm under a lot of pressure to win, so fewer players makes it easier to score gold.) Yet as the rest of the events heated up, I found myself wondering if they were ever going to get into the game.

To be fair, the Sibling Summer Olympics is no ordinary spectator sport. The rules and regs are often a bit confusing for a newcomer.

One of the more challenging elements is that the players are also the judges. They each have their own set of scoring criteria, and, in many cases, their own set of events. So while one family may think they're trying to win the "Whose kids can show the most initiative on the Wave Runner?" trophy, another family is hotly pursuing the "Best manners at the dinner table" crown.

The scoring itself is highly subjective. Huddled conferences among judges establish strategic alliances that change each day and sometimes each hour. And much like Olympic ice skating, people from your own region are judged by one set of criteria, but competitors from somewhere else, anywhere else, are judged by completely different standards.

Of course, it should also be noted that the rules have never been documented in any sort of playbook. The judging criteria is actually communicated via the facial expressions and body language of the other judges/competitors.

However, no one ever really knows where they stand in the point total because the scores are tallied each night via whispered pillow talk between spouses, and each set of judges/competitors comes up with their own rankings.

To make matters even more complicated, those said judges/competitors have also been known to jump in as coaches when other teams fall behind.

You wouldn't think such fierce rivals would want to give in to their opponents. But since we're all really such helpful people, even though we desperately want the win, we can't bear to watch another team flounder. So we often provide useful pointers on how they might improve their performance. We know they can't win, but we don't want to watch them losing too badly.

Since the coaching is typically done on a volunteer basis, the other players often don't even realize that someone from the opposing team is trying to help them out. Being polite and all, we don't like providing direct feedback or shouting suggestions from the sidelines. So our performance tips are usually offered as innocuous comments delivered from behind a thin veneer of Southern manners.

"Are you sure John Jr. should be eating all those pickles?"

"Dang, every time I go into the bathroom the toilet paper roll is on backward."

"Wow, your kids sure do like television."

To the untrained ear, these remarks sound like pleasant conversations. Yet these statements are actually warnings about potential point deductions. If you act upon them quickly, your score will remain intact. But if you choose to ignore the coaching, you not only lose points for your original error, but you lose additional points for failing to correct yourself after you have been cited for your mistake.

This year, the award for Best in Show was a wide-open race. Whether the category was "Correct kitchen cleanup," "Most efficient, electronic, life-management system," or "Best parent–child interaction"—we all wanted to win.

Well, at least those of us who knew we were playing wanted to win. But we were certain that with enough demonstration, the others would eventually catch on and join in the fun.

My own team, consisting of myself, my husband, and our two kids, started off strong, and I believe we won the "Who can bring the most junk?" round. But then we lost big-time in the "Who can make a big point of reading to their kids every night?" event. (Other teams considered this a compulsory event, but since we think it's an optional round for away games, we're not counting that score into our total). I'm pretty sure we pulled ahead in the "Let's show everyone how a less compulsive parent handles a bug bite" competition. And I know for certain my husband smoked 'em all in the "Who can eat the most Cheetos and still have room for dinner?" challenge.

However, as the week wore on, the rigors of competition began to take their toll. Teams that had once been humming performance machines began to crack under the pressure. And as the imported spouses became increasingly aware of the daily scoring, they started sniping at their fellow team captains (a.k.a. their husbands or wives).

My own husband quit being an all-round player and decided that beer drinking was going to be his one and only event.

To make matters even worse, my starting lineup, namely my two daughters, began whining during critical moments of the competition. My youngest completely choked on the "Who can go down for their nap without complaining?" round. And if I didn't know better, I would've thought my eldest was trying to throw the race when she blatantly refused to get into the starting block for the "How many math facts can you recite at one sitting?" event.

Yet, despite the weary, unmotivated spouses, the complaining children, and continuing crazy rule changes, my siblings and I were determined to tough out the competition until the bitter end.

But what finally pushed us over the edge and threw the entire Sibling Summer Olympics into utter chaos was the realization that our parents, who for years had been the final authority on which events were important and what the real scoring criteria was, had decided to abandon their job as head officials.

They didn't publicly announce that they were quitting. But they made snippy little comments like "You're all adults now, so whatever works best for each of you is fine," which led us to believe they were no longer willing to referee the games.

My father, a man who once mediated a fight about how to slice a Twizzler into three equal parts and who often reminded us that "Whatever you do out there in the world reflects on this family," actually said one night at dinner, "It's so nice to enjoy you all without having to feel responsible for everything you do."

Had they gone mad? Clearly the man's arthritis was affecting his mind.

A rivalry as fierce as this one, that's taken us from fighting over Popsicle sticks to drawing a line across the back seat of our Buick to comparing 401Ks cannot be quelled by simpering edicts like, "It's so great that you're all so different."

What the heck is the point of holding a Sibling Summer Olympics if your parents refuse to declare a winner?

I swear, if my folks didn't own the boat and buy the beer, I might be tempted to boycott these games altogether. As it is, I don't see how the Sibling Summer Olympics can survive with no one to referee the action. How are we supposed to settle scoring disputes if there is no head official? Do these people actually think we're just going to call this thing a draw and go home?

I suppose a more mature woman might elect to retire gracefully and leave the thrill of competition for the next generation. But as the eldest, I've been anticipating my victory lap for so long that I can't concede until the game is won.

If the rest of my family would just give up and award me the gold, perhaps we could skip the Sibling Summer Olympics and take a vacation instead. But until I hear the cheers and feel that medal around my neck, I'm going to keep training for next year.

The Little Fat Ballerina

James Whorton Jr.

Audrey got offered a job in Kingsport, Tennessee, for four times what Tim had been making in Atlanta, so they moved. Now it would be Tim not working, and therefore it must be Tim packing the child's lunch and getting her up and dressed and driving her to preschool, also chauffeuring her to Story Time at the library and ice cream after that if she had been good. He could hardly complain, for how many times in their old life had he sat watching *Hardball* and drinking his nightly dose of bourbon while dishes were being washed and the three-year-old entertained in the very next room? That was when he'd been the breadwinner, coming home tired. Now this.

He enrolled Emily at Miss Nadia's School of Dance for a nine-week ballet course and was given a list of required apparel: ballet slippers, plain leotard in white or pink, plain white or pink tights. On Wednesday afternoon he took his daughter to an old brick building with a fire escape on it in downtown Kingsport. Inside, he held her hand as they climbed two flights of stairs then emerged into the middle of a large, wood-floored loft where different ages of girls were wandering about with different amounts of clothes on. There was no clear center to the activity: mothers fussed over daughters here and there, and clusters of older girls would run out from one side room then disappear into another. Tim led Emily to a bench by the wall and produced from the bag they had been kept in all week her new ballet slippers. She had not been allowed to play in them at home. A glassy bead of drool fell from her mouth onto the side of his hand as he slid the second slipper onto her foot and tied the small elastic drawstring in a tight bow. She often drooled when something had her closest attention, and Tim thought nothing of drying his hand with a swipe on the leg of his jeans. Fatherhood had wrecked the fine fastidiousness that he had cherished, once.

A woman in a black bodysuit called for the three-year-olds. Tim led Emily over. The woman wrote out Emily's name in marker on a sticker which she stuck on Emily's chest. Class began, in one of the side rooms, with the door shut. But there was a large window, mirrored on the inside, through which the mothers and Tim could watch.

The girls sat on a mat with their legs stretched out in front of them. The teacher went down the line touching each girl on the head. When she came to Emily, she knelt and pulled Emily's toes, showing her how to arch her foot.

The audience of mothers thinned out. Some paired off chattering, and others just disappeared, so that soon only Tim was left observing with a somewhat uncomfortable pressure in his throat as his beautiful daughter frowned with concentration, studying her teacher's movements and those of the other girls, trying to twist her knees out in first position. Tim had brushed her hair and done his very damnedest to put it in a bun as the handout had instructed. Emily's hair was thin, and he did not know how to use bobby pins correctly. Her bun looked like a meatball rolled in sphagnum moss.

He could have wept for love of his daughter, but didn't, at this moment. He did not understand why he was the only parent watching. These other chattering mothers were like the people on airplanes who keep their nose in a paperback while outside the window, the face of the planet is spread out naked. The failure of such people to be moved was beyond him and even annoyed him somewhat.

Then toward the end of class, two of the other instructors came to the glass to watch. One was an older woman who had frizzy orange hair with gray roots and who spoke with what sounded like a bona fide Russian accent. This must be the notorious Miss Nadia. According to the brochure she had danced with the St. Petersburg Ballet, and according to Tim and Audrey's realtor she was an extremely exacting teacher—the only one worth considering in Kingsport, if a girl were serious about ballet.

Tim eavesdropped. "That one's good. Look at her hands," Miss Nadia said.

He knew the one she meant—he'd noticed her too, a slender-necked beauty who held her hands just so.

"The little fat ones will never make dancers, however."

Tim thought he must have heard wrong. "Excuse me?" he said.

Miss Nadia blinked at him. "What?"

"Did I hear you say what I thought I heard you say?"

"That couldn't be," Miss Nadia said. "Because I wasn't speaking to you."

Class ended and Tim's daughter ran out and threw both arms around his knees. He waddled to the bench by the wall, and when he got her loose from his legs and was tying her sneakers back on, she said, "Daddy, I love ballet."

*

"I want to bomb her house," Tim told Audrey that night.

Audrey stared at him. Was she weighing what he had told her, or was she thinking of something else? They were in the kitchen, the child upstairs in bed on schedule.

"Where can I get a bomb? I'm talking about a real one. I want to put a Stinger missile in her house."

"I mean, she's right," Audrey said. "There are no fat ballerinas."

Tim began listing the reasons why Miss Nadia's comment was unacceptable to him and should also be unacceptable to Audrey.

Audrey cut him off. "You know what? Stop being so angry. I've been listening to angry men go on all day."

Tim was speechless. He got his keys, walked back through

the kitchen so Audrey would see that he had his keys, and left shutting the door quietly so as not to wake the child.

He drove aimlessly around Kingsport, seething at first but soon settling down. A quality of Audrey's that probably made her useful as a junior attorney for a large chemical corporation but which at the same time made her infuriating to live with was her habit of always seeing another side to the matter. The proper reaction to an insult to one's child is anger and resentment, Tim thought. Of course there was another side to it, but did that observation have to be the first thing out of Audrey's mouth?

It was difficult for Tim, he considered, adjusting to this new life with no job other than looking after his daughter. Yes, he brought his full modicum of testosterone to the task. He was testy about his daughter's weight, about her baby fat that had lasted longer than some other girls' had. Her diet was OK. Sometimes in the afternoon when he wanted some peace he would park her in front of the TV with a snack for an hour and a half of golden quiet time.

At a stop light on Ft. Henry Drive a woman pulled up alongside him in a Jeep. She looked maybe 30, her hair pulled back in a bouncy ponytail. The lighting from the bright parking lots all around them, from the CVS drugstore and the Exxon and the Food City supermarket, was sufficient to let him see that her cheeks were blotchy with healthy color, as though she were perhaps on her way home from a good workout at the gym. He had occasionally wished that it were possible for him to carry a sign in his car that said "YOU'RE PRETTY" on it. He could flash his sign then drive off—nothing creepy, just a way to let a person know she'd been appreciated, that she'd been fallen in love with for a few seconds there, before he vanished harmlessly from her life. He imagined the sign made out of stiff paperboard with a flat wooden handle glued to it. A doctor's tongue depressor would be ideal.

Coming home he saw his neighbors' trash bins along the street and was reminded to wheel his out too. These were enormous plastic containers with heavy flip-top lids. The garbage truck had a robot arm that lifted and emptied them. Under the streetlight Tim swung the lid back to make sure a scavenging possum had not gotten trapped inside. His 90-year-old neighbor Mr. Deadrick had warned him that this could happen. No possum tonight.

In the house, he found Audrey on the sofa playing Free Cell on her laptop while she watched a movie on the *Independent Film Channel* and ate goldfish crackers from a bowl. He sat down beside her.

Audrey was very fast at Free Cell. From time to time she would click on the wrong stack of cards, only because her finger was moving so fast on the touch pad, and then the computer would make an error noise, something like *BLABLONK!* To Tim it was a not uncomforting sound. He found the remote and hit the Info button to get himself caught up on the movie.

*

Tim tried earnestly to talk Emily into giving up ballet, or at least into quitting Miss Nadia's School of Dance. Emily was a funny kid sometimes. When he told her he wanted to switch her to another school, she said nothing, which he took for acquiescence. Then a minute later, when he was talking about something else, the corners of her mouth turned down, and she whispered that she would never see Miss Nicole again. Miss Nicole was the instructor for the three-year-olds, the one who had pulled on Emily's toes. How could Emily have formed the attachment so quickly? Anyway, Tim did not have the stomach for this fight, and therefore next Wednesday he found himself back on the third floor of the same brick building in downtown Kingsport tying his daughter's slippers then watching her dash off into the classroom to stand very straight and solemn while attempting to point her feet out to the sides. She was knock-kneed. Back in Atlanta, he had pointed this out to the pediatrician, who assured him with a laugh that it was very common in girls Emily's age. Emily was "a little past where we want her to be on the weight chart," the pediatrician added, "but I don't like to lay too much emphasis on that early in a girl's life because some parents become obsessive about a daughter's weight, and that can lead to much worse issues later on." Translation: Tim was himself a potential threat to his daughter's emotional well-being.

"I just want her to be healthy in every way," Tim told the pediatrician, and in return he received something he enjoyed very much, an approving smile from his daughter's physician. Actually Dr. Menendez was a resident, so maybe not a full-fledged physician yet, but she had a lot of sense in Tim's estimation and was also rather breathtaking with her glossy long brown hair and her white lab coat with the stethoscope in the pocket.

Today, after a few minutes watching his daughter's class at the window, he sat down. One of the mothers was reading a magazine nearby, and he sized her up with a glance. Thirty, glasses, educated; dress made of purple burlap; hair cut close to her head but with longer, wispy locks down her neck and around her ears. Very pale-complected—avoided meat on principle, no doubt. He was meaning to look away when she looked up at him.

"It is nice to see one father here," she said.

"Oh! My wife is working, so—" He blathered on with little idea of what he was saying. Somehow he got around to Miss Nadia's comment.

The woman's mouth dropped open. "She said that? Really?"

"Yes! Not to me, but I overheard it. She said, 'The fat ones will never make dancers.'"

"I can't believe it!"

Tim was satisfied. This was the reaction he had expected from Emily's mother. The correct reaction.

"Well, we're doing it, but ballet is horrible stuff," the woman said. She had freckles, Tim noticed. Lots of them, on her face, neck, and arms. "Read *Anna Karenina*. The ballerinas are all courtesans."

Tim smiled. "I'm not likely to read *Anna Karenina*," he said.

"You should. It's a wonderful novel."

"I like to read books on how to do things, or history, or maybe something comical. Something I can get some use out of."

The woman smiled tolerantly, as though she understood his masculine impatience with the laid-back world of novel-reading. She did not immediately pick up her magazine again. They sat quietly for a pleasant moment. She reached down into her capacious handbag—it could have passed for a Pony Express-style saddlebag, really—and brought out a small tube from which she unscrewed the cap and squeezed out some cream into her palm. She rubbed the cream into her hands, taking special care with the knuckles. The right hand rubbed the knuckles of the left hand, and then the reverse.

"You're pretty," Tim blurted out.

The hand rubbing ceased while she raised one eyebrow slightly. She nodded once.

"Whoa," Tim said. "Where did that come from? Oops."

With a composure that suggested she would now place the authoritative and final interpretation on the odd event that had just taken place between them, she shifted slightly away from him, and saying nothing, she picked up her magazine and resumed browsing in it.

Was it a crime? Did a law forbid Tim's telling a freckled woman she was pretty even though they were strangers and he was married? Not quite! Also, if he had been trying to "pick her up," he would not have attempted this in such a clumsy and idiotic manner at the ballet school.

Still, in the world he lived in, it wasn't done. Men who say such things are the pitiful fodder of sexual harassment seminars like the ones Tim and all his coworkers had been required to attend every year in his old job, back when he had one. Except for wives and girlfriends, telling women they are pretty is considered to be an impertinence. There is no acceptable way to express the sentiment no matter how harmlessly intended. It was a thought that had to be kept to oneself! OK to think, but not OK to say! Shut up Tim!

After ballet, Tim took Emily to Dairy Queen for a dip-top. The form of this marvelously engineered food product put him in mind of the domes of St. Basil's Cathedral, another great fruit of the Russian culture along with Miss Nadia and the novels of Tolstoy. A boy at the drive-through passed the cone to Tim in his car, and Tim passed it to back to his daughter, strapped snugly in her child restraint seat.

On the road he nudged the rearview mirror down, so he could see her. She was holding the cone just looking at it.

"You need to bite the tip off, so you can get to the ice cream," he said.

"You do it," she said, and at a red light he twisted in his seat and took the cone. A fine misty sheen had condensed from the hot summer air on the cool brown waxy shell. He topped it and passed it back to her as the light turned green. He drove.

She caught him still eyeing her in the mirror. "Daddy, I love my dip-top," she said.

This pleased him, because he too had once loved dip-tops very much. He was not able to enjoy them with the old keenness anymore. Why? He was too distracted, perhaps. Once, far back in a time of his life which he could recall now only in bright smudgy fragments, he had been able to really concentrate on his ice cream. The result had been a happiness as pure as you like.

Because of her gorgeousness and also the sticky mess she was creating in the back seat, he couldn't take his eyes off his daughter in the mirror. Finally, rather than have a wreck and kill them both, he pulled into a post office parking lot, so he could turn around and marvel at her safely.

FROM THE LONG HOME

WILLIAM GAY

Several years back William Tell Oliver had gone out to his hoglot one morning and found a curious phenomenon. He had kept a few sows and a boar then and what he saw so surprised him that he set the bucket of feed he was carrying aside and stood leaning against the fence, ignoring the riotous squealing of the pigs, just staring out at the lot.

There were two holes there, craters almost, ovals roughly five or six feet in diameter and almost two feet deep. After a time the old man climbed the fence and passed among the milling hogs and inspected the holes closely, expecting who knew what. They were a wonder to him. He squatted in the offal of the lot examining them. The manure and rich black earth mounded their rims and the bottoms were smooth. He peered closely at the bottoms, perhaps looking for the remnants of some molten star, thin, bright layers of celestial slag. Hurled here at random or by discernment.

There was nothing. Only the dark earth beneath the layered manure and what he took to be spade marks. "Be damned," he said to himself. With his walking stick to part the thick weeds about the fence he searched for signs. He had no idea what he expected to find. Old bones replevied from the curious graves, new bodies so destined. All he found was the hot ferment of the weeds and a copperhead moving sleek and burnished in search of deeper shade. He let his mind wander. What would there be to steal? He counted the hogs three times and all three times they were all accounted for. "What else in a piglot," he asked himself, "save pigs and pigshit? A manure thief?" He looked for tiretracks without expecting to find them, for there was no road through the weeds and his mind could conceive of no one so desperate for pigshit they must steal it under cover of darkness and cart it away on their backs.

It was a mystery and he didn't care for mysteries: an old man who suspected chaos and disorder beyond the curtain of swirling dark, he hungered for order and symmetry in what remained of his life, a balancing of the scales.

He fed and watered the hogs and returned to the house. When his chores were completed he sat for a time in the shade of a pear tree, his eyes closed, feet up on a Coke crate, listening to the drone of bees glutting themselves on the ripe and windfallen fruit. Before the day was over he had returned to the lot to puzzle anew over the holes. He learned no more than the nothing he already knew.

In the morning there were three new holes, somewhat shallower but spaced over a wider area, as if someone had been digging for something at random. "Be damned," he said again. He stared at the harried earth, suspecting perhaps some magnetic anomaly that sucked meteors and asteroids from the dusty band of space he hurtled through. He stared upward, seeking some cosmic mirror whose reflections marvelously cast chaos into order, righted the perverse and disordered, but he peered only into blue emptiness, past shapeless wisps of clouds that fled westward ahead of the sun. He stood listening to the morning sounds that mocked him with their familiarity. He could hear the crinkling of hot tin, the pop of barn rafters warping in the heat. The furtive scuttling of a lizard. A thin film of perspiration crept across his shoulders, dampening his chambray shirt.

He counted the pigs again without expecting to find one gone. They were all there and he was halfdisappointed, surprised to find himself willing to sacrifice a pig for an explanation. A pig thief he could have understood, there was reason in it, sense. There was no sense in these holes pitting his hoglot. After awhile he got a manure fork and began halfheartedly to shovel the earth back into the holes.

He took a long nap that afternoon and about dark he made himself a quart jar of coffee and carried it with him down to the barn. He had an old Browning over-and-under and he carried that too. In the hayloft he arranged bales of hay into a comfortable chair and settled himself out of sight to see what transpired.

For a long time nothing did. Dark deepened and shadows took the world. He sat immersed in the cries of insects, in the timeless tolling of whippoorwills. There was something of eternity in these sounds, at once bitter and reassuring. He'd heard them as a boy, as a young man, they sounded the same then as now. In this curiously altered stillness he felt he might even hear his wife open the kitchen door and call his name, his son might be on the spring path following him, a small form forever stalemated by time. He drank from the jar of bitter coffee and wiped his mouth on a sleeve, forced his attention to the barnyard below him. It lay in darkness but after an hour or so the moon cradled up out of the eastern trees and the pale illumination crept across the face of the land, tree and fence and stone imbued with significance like images in a dream.

The moon was high over the treeline and he judged it ten o'clock or better before he saw anything stir. When the boy came he came up from the branch-run with silent stealth, easing through the border of gum and persimmon, peering all about, cautious as a grazing deer. Apparently satisfied, he came out of the brush and approached the fence, carrying a burlap bag and a shovel whose handle was longer than he was tall. It was the Hodges boy. Why, he ain't no morn nine or ten years old, he thought. The boy threw the sack over and leaned the shovel against the fence and clambered over. He took up the shovel and immediately fell to work, selecting a fresh corner of the lot to dig in. Just clock in and go to work, the old man thought in puzzlement. The boy dug for some time and then unpocketed a flashlight, knelt on the scattered manure he'd dug from the hole, raking carefully through it with his hands. Kneeling so in the earth he raised his face to a moon clocking on westward and then arose and commenced shoveling again.

The old man was at a loss. For a moment he thought of Hodges's grandfather digging for money on the Mormon place, perhaps some genetic quirk had encoded it in the third generation, a trait so degenerated by now that nothing remained save the compulsion to dig at random just on the offchance someone might have buried something worth replevying.

Oliver rose as stealthily as he could, even so his knees popped and he stood still and silent until he saw the boy hadn't heard. Then he moved cautiously toward the ladder and climbed down it. When he eased into the moonlit piglot Hodges was still digging. Oliver approached within a foot or so of his back. "Hidy," he said. The boy dropped the shovel as if electricity had coursed through it and leapt five or six inches into the air. When his feet touched earth they were already pedaling as if he rode an invisible bicycle and he was almost immediately at the fence. Oliver caught him as he was scrambling over the topmost slab and lifted him, kicking and squirming and cursing, and set him back to earth.

"Let me alone," the boy was yelling.

"Whoa, young feller. Hold on a minute here. Nobody aims to hurt you. I just want to know what you're up to."

Hodges was trying to jerk his arm free. "None of your Goddamn business. Now, let me alone."

"You're young Hodges, ain't ye?"

"What's it to ye?"

"Well, they don't call ye Hodges, do they? What's ye first name?"

"Yeah, I guess you'd like that, wouldn't ye? Me tell ye my name so's you could run straight to the law with it."

"Hell, son, I don't need no name. I got you in the flesh, right by the seat of the britches. I'se just askin to be polite."

"My name's Clifford."

"All right. That's some better. And just so you'll know, I ain't never been one to run overquick to the law. Now, you reckon if I turn you aloose you can control the impulse to jump that fence?"

"I ain't done nothin."

"You move right pert for a feller just takin the night air. Ain't none too qualmy about these copperheads neither." Oliver released his grip on the boy. "Now, what's my hoglot got you can't dig up nowheres else?"

"Wouldn't you like to know?"

Oliver had been wanting to smoke but had been afraid of setting the hay in the barnloft afire. Now he packed the bowl of his pipe and struck a kitchen match on his thumbnail and lit the tobacco. When he spoke his voice was furred by the smoke. "What was you digging for?"

"It ain't none of your business."

"Well. I reckon it's your shovel. But it's my lot and my hogs been standin around losin sleep and watchin you diggin like a fool. Now, what is it? Do you just like diggin or is there somethin particular about my hoglot that appeals to you?"

The boy seemed to be considering, there was a shrewdness

to his features, a transparent cunning. Oliver watched the play of thoughts on the small freckled face. Half is better than nothing, the face was thinking. Oliver grinned. The face was already trying to devise a plan for cheating him out of his half of whatever it was he didn't even know about yet.

"Well. I guess we could split."

"I don't see why not."

The boy squatted on the earth before him. In the moonlight they were dwarfed by the dark shapes of trees above them. A warm wind smelling of summer going overripe came looping up the hollow and across them. Faint surcease scented with rich opulence, the ripe pears and musk of honeysuckle. An owl called lonesome from a hollow negated by dark.

"Well. It's pigs."

"Pigs?" the old man asked in disbelief.

"Hell, yeah. I'd a thought a man as old as you are would have figured it out hisself by now."

"Boy, you've lost me. Figured out what?"

"Diggin up them pigs."

Oliver felt like a participant in some surreal conversation in which the answers bore no relation to the questions, lines had been fragmented and shuffled indiscriminately. "They Godamighty. Is that what you been doin out here of a night? And them sacks..."

Hodges was nodding. "To tote em home in," he said.

"Lord God, boy. You don't dig pigs up out of the ground like taters or somethin."

"You want em all for yeself," the boy said craftily.

"Whoever told you pigs was dug?"

"My mama did and I don't know what cause she'd have to lie."

"I see," Oliver said.

"I ast her where they come from and she said the old sow rooted em up in the hogpen."

"And you not havin a hogpen..."

He sat in a ruminative silence, just smoking the pipe and listening to the crying of the nightbirds, somewhere far and lost and streaking down the night the whistle of a train. "And what'd you figure, just kindly eliminate the sow? Bypass her sort of? Just dig the pigs up ahead of her and sell em?"

"Yeah. A person's smartern a hog ain't he?"

"We won't argue about it," Oliver said. "I suspect folks listening to us might work up evidence for either side."

He sat watching the boy. This diminutive hog rustler, self-confessed and unrepentant thief of unborn swine. He with his fallow burlap bags and eye cocked to livestock futures. Oliver saw little that was lovable. He had a moment of clairvoyance, an insight of weary foreknowledge stabbed with regret. He knew that Clifford Hodges would always be slipping in at night and digging up somebody else's pigs. He would always be playing the longshot or taking a shortcut, figuring the angles in somebody else's game. And he would never have a game of his own. If he lived until he was grown he would be shot then or shoot someone else in a failed inept holdup. He and a cohort halfmad as they looked aghast at each other across the body of a fallen grocer or gaspump operator. If he won the game he'd be in Brushy Mountain penitentiary, if he lost the graveyard.

Oliver felt a pity for him, a commiseration for the things that had been and things that were yet to be. He wished for words to encourage him, to enlighten him, but none came. And his own life did not lend itself to examples.

"Well, what about it?"

"What about what?"

"About them pigs. Are we goin to split like we said or are you goin to dig em up after I leave and keep em for yeself?"

"Boy, they ain't no pigs there to dig."

"You done got em."

"Goddamn it. Son, that ain't where pigs comes from. I done told you that."

"So you say."

"Well, there's a considerable body of evidence to back it up."

"Then where does the old sow get em?"

Oliver took a deep breath. "All right," he said. "They grow there in the sow. Then when they're big enough, when they're made, they come out."

"Come out," the boy echoed. He was shaking his head, staring at Oliver in wonderment. "Everbody says you're crazy and by God you are," he said. "You're crazy as hell. I never heard such a crock of bullshit in my life."

"Well," the old man said, "don't blame me for it. It's not like I laid it out or anything. It's always been like that."

"I'm goin to tell Mama," Hodges said. He arose and took up the burlap bag and the shovel and hurled them over the fence and clambered after them. "Keep ye damn pigs," he said. "I don't mind ye being greedy but I hate to be took for a fool."

Oliver grinned to himself. "You watch for snakes," he called. After awhile he could hear Hodges scurrying down the embankment, a small bright angry thread in the pastoral tapestry of night sounds. He hunkered still in the barnlot awhile listening and then he arose and went on back toward the house.

Bit Part

Tom Franklin

On the way to the party, Laura advises me not to drink too much.

"And don't get starstruck," she tells me, "or compliment anybody. You've got to act like you're an 'us,' or you're out. You can't behave like a 'them.'"

She hugs a curve with her white Miata and downshifts as we climb another hill, the famous HOLLYWOOD sign spread out below us, its scaffolding dank and unimpressive from the rear. More dips and climbs, and finally Laura stabs her brakes and parallel parks by a tall, white stucco wall, imposing and covered with ivy. On the other side is Kevin Costner's house.

"Do I look okay?" I ask her.

She takes off her sunglasses and appraises my worn blue jeans and white button-down. "Untuck the shirt."

We get buzzed in the gate and walk past a guest house, where Costner's assistant waves us through. The main house, same stucco and ivy as the wall, is huge and sectional, rambling like enormous steps down the rocky, wooded hill. We go into the opened front door, past fifteen or twenty suitcases along the wall, and soon I'm holding a Corona and doing my best "us" act, talking to Garry Shandling in the kitchen. When I say I love *The Larry Sanders Show,* he smiles.

"This is your first one of these parties, right?"

"Is it obvious?" I tell him I'm from Alabama, out here visiting Laura for the weekend.

"Just realize," he says, "that this isn't a typical Hollywood party. This is a Hollywood Leading Man party."

"What's the difference?"

"You'll see," Shandling says. A tan, long-legged blond in a bikini top and shorts shimmies up to him, and he turns to her.

So I'm off, wandering from room to room, alone, too shy to join any of the groups of good-looking people who talk and laugh and refuse my friendly eye-contact. Instead, I try to appear interested in the décor, examine each painting and potted plant. Everyone here wears sunglasses, even inside, so I put on mine. They introduce themselves by first names—"I'm Garry"—so I plan to start doing that, too.

I go out the sliding door to the upstairs deck, where Laura has her face to the sun. She fits right in here, among the beautiful people. At home I have a videotape full of television shows she's been on: *Friends, Nash Bridges, The Pretender, Fantasy Island.* She's done dozens of commercials and won small roles in movies, too: *Enemy of the State* and *For Love of the Game.* We met in grad school in Mobile nearly ten years ago, but I'm under orders not to reveal this because she doesn't want anyone to know she has her master's degree—intelligence might hinder her from getting auditions. I'm also not to mention her age. If anybody asks, she's twenty-five.

From the deck, you can see across the lush valley to mansions half hidden by trees and foliage, dark windows, sparkle of sun off clear pool water. I sit on the wall and sip my Corona.

Suddenly Costner approaches me, wearing cargo shorts and no shirt, his face glistening with sunblock. He looks exactly like he does in his movies, all of which I've seen, even *Fandango*.

"You're Laura's friend," he says, smiling. "I'm Kevin."

I stand, and we shake hands. "Tom," I say.

"You want to borrow some swim trunks?"

I almost say yes, but a vision of my pale, freckled, slumped shoulders and potbelly brings me to my senses. "No, thanks," I say, and Costner smiles again and goes down the steps.

I replay the conversation in my head, trying to revise the three words I said into something intelligent and interesting. I've always loved movies, spent the weekends of my youth in the local drive-in and the rest of my time in front of the television. As an adult, I'll sometimes see two, three movies a day. And now it feels like I've stepped into a movie myself—here comes Jon Lovitz wearing Bermuda shorts and his trademark goofy smile, heading down the row of stone steps to a swimming pool filled with dark-skinned, big-chested women. Then a small, old, very, very, *very* tan man—practically a charred skeleton—passes me in a Speedo, a towel around his neck. He descends the steps and, as he nears the pool, women rise to meet him.

"Who's that guy?" I ask Laura as she comes out the sliding door.

She squints against the sun. "Exec producer." She names his most recent film.

"Wow," I say.

Below, Costner is propped on his elbows on a towel by the pool, between two gorgeous women in bikinis, their straps down. Women are everywhere. Even the one who's constantly cleaning up—the maid—is a beauty.

"Models," Laura says. "And what do they have in common? Aspirations and boob jobs."

"Really? All of them?"

"The only real breasts at this party are under my shirt." She winks. "But don't tell anybody."

A wet woman in a thong comes up the steps wringing water from her hair. Laura introduces me as her "best friend from forever." I want her to say, *This is my friend Tom. He's a writer. He wrote a book called* Poachers, *which will be published in a couple of months. He's very interesting and smart and funny.* Instead, she says, "He's from Alabama."

"No kidding," the model says. "I think Charlotte's from there, too. Wait." She heads off. Soon she's back, dragging yet another beautiful woman, this one in a grass skirt and cowboy hat, and we're left alone.

"So," I say, "what part of Alabama?"

"Birmingham," she says as she walks away, skirt rustling.

Which is fine. I wouldn't want to talk to me, either. If I were her, I'd get next to Kevin Costner. "*Bull Durham* was great!" I'd say. "I loved *The Untouchables.*"

I find Laura again, standing in the kitchen, which has gotten crowded. I touch my shoulder to hers so she'll know I'm here. Everyone's laughing at something David Spade is saying. I laugh, too. Then suddenly, Costner walks in the door wearing jeans and a short-sleeved shirt, no shoes. My peripheral vision tracks him. There are three or four clusters of people in the room, and I notice that each one sort of adjusts for him, makes a little space on the outside edge nearest him. I feel myself adjusting, too—*Hey Kevin, pick us.* Spade is still talking, and we laugh to order, but Costner joins a group led by the tan producer. Our group sags a little, but Spade pushes on intrepidly.

I'm beginning to get it: In this Hollywood Leading Man party, Costner is the star. Shandling, Lovitz, and Spade have supporting roles. Laura and the models get one or two lines each, maybe a nude scene. But me, I'm just an extra, Short Pale Guy at Pool, condemned to speechlessness. Unless, of course, I can somehow snag a bigger role. Plus, there's this voice in my head going, *Pitch him your book.*

"What can I say to get Costner's attention?" I whisper to Laura.

"Anything but 'I'm your biggest fan.'"

So I'm off, skulking around the giant kitchen, the butcher-block island, the bar, casually examining the appliances and bottles of booze and bowls of tortilla chips, trying to anticipate which cluster Costner will join. When I choose the one I think he'll pick, I attach myself to it, but he joins another group. After three rounds of this, I give up.

"He's avoiding me," I tell Laura.

I expect her to call me paranoid, but she says, "Maybe it's because you're with me. He probably thinks you're my date."

"You mean, he's jealous of me?"

"No, he's Kevin Costner. He's not 'jealous' of anybody. But he may see himself in *competition* with you."

Costner's going for the refrigerator. I give Laura's arm a squeeze and move to intercept.

"Great party, Kevin," I say, raising my beer with my left hand so he'll see the wedding ring.

"Thanks," he says. "Enjoy yourself."

I'm about to tell him that my wife loves his work, a flat-out lie, as she rarely watches movies, but he's gone already, joining Spade's group. They all laugh.

"He blew me off," I tell Laura.

"Tell him you like the way he's decorated the house."

"Great décor, Kev," I say the next time, again flashing my ring, as he heads out the door.

"Thanks, man," he says. "Have Tim give you the tour."

Tim is the tall blond guy in charge of the party. Sort of like a bouncer, and one of Costner's oldest friends, I've noticed him watching me, probably trying to gauge whether I'm truly an "us." I introduce myself, and he guides me around the house: Costner's son's bedroom (complete with *Waterworld* pinball machine), Costner's two-story closet (four racks of suits, all Armani), the dark basement theater room with a dozen or so seats and a twelve-foot screen. Here, behind bars on a black shelf, are Costner's two Oscars, for *Dances with Wolves*.

"Go ahead," Tim says. "Pick 'em up."

I reach through and take one around the waist and lift it. Very heavy. I notice that, with the statue in hand, you can't remove it from between the bars.

When we finish the tour, it's darker outside. Everyone has started to change into evening wear, which explains all the suitcases by the door. The cleaning lady, now in a sequined, sleeveless blouse and short skirt, is restocking the refrigerator with Corona and Heineken.

"That's the best-looking maid I've ever seen," I tell Laura.

"She's not the maid. She's a model."

"Why is she cleaning?"

Laura smiles and sucks a lime. "She's putting out the domestic vibe for Kevin."

Aspirations and boobs. It's one big audition, I think. All about what you can offer, and all I have is a collection of stories.

More people arrive, Tia Carrere with entourage. More producers. More models. Shandling—now in khaki shorts and a denim shirt—is reclining on a sofa talking to Charlotte, Spade to a woman nearly twice his height. Models flit everywhere, their bikinis gone in favor of capri pants, short skirts, strapless dresses. A cook is grilling chicken breasts on the side deck. A projectionist arrives with the cased reels of a movie not yet showing in theaters and screens it in the basement. Outside, a model flashes a producer, and they clink beer bottles—a deal settled? Another model kicks off her sandals, then tees golf balls and rockets them over the valley below while men cheer. And while they cheer, she stuffs two of the balls inside her white mesh top, like large nipples.

I tuck my shirt in, hoping it'll appear I've changed clothes, and walk around nursing my Corona, lurking in corners, circling the kitchen, waiting for Costner—now wearing a pressed white Armani shirt—so I can talk to him. *Do I have a book for you. There's a character, a game warden, who's perfect. . .*

But Costner settles on the balcony outside his bedroom, surrounded by ferns and women, and I never get my chance. The rest of us sit on the rails and watch. Except to say goodnight and shake hands, Costner and I don't speak again. The next day I fly home to Mobile, coach.

*

When it's published two months later, I send Laura a copy of my book, inscribed to Costner: "I hope you like these stories."

The next time I call her, I ask if she gave him the collection.

"Yes."

"Did he read it?"

She doesn't think so, but says she saw it lying on his bedside table.

In my mind, I attend another Hollywood Leading Man party, this time as Screenwriter of the New Costner Flick. There I am, reclining in a Speedo by the pool—tan, svelte, coiffed—smiling at Shandling as he tells me he loves my script. And on the deck you can see Charlotte, trying to screw up her courage to approach me—*I'm from Alabama, too!* And there, across the clear water of the pool, stands Kevin Costner himself, raising his Corona in tribute. Behind my sunglasses I smile and give him a thumbs-up while music plays and the dollars roll in and Laura and all the lovely women of the world waft by, auditioning.

Meat-Smoking Son of a Gun

David Magee

I call them redneckosexuals, the small percentage of today's young Southern males who feel that—by virtue of significant, six-figure earnings and a sort of über-hipness learned from metropolitan travel and hyper-shopping and fashion-conscious wives—they have the world by the tail, moving it and grooving it however and whenever. It's a blend of rural, generational toughness and soft, cosmopolitan self-enlightenment, dwelling in cities like Atlanta, Jacksonville, Memphis, Mobile, Nashville, Birmingham and the like.

The opposite of Manhattan's metrosexual male, who can rarely be identified by testosterone traits, the South's contemporary hip-billy is part Jethro and John Wayne mixed with an equal portion of Paris Hilton and Madonna. These men are just as liable to sneak off from work early on a Friday to hunt ducks as they are to get a slight permanent and dye job for wilting, withering hair.

This young, savvy Southern male likely works as either a litigant lawyer, a specialist doctor, commodities broker, real estate developer, or as a chairman's son inheritor, working out at the gym on his muscle tone during the lunch hour, sucking down three beers with the boys at the neighborhood bar during Happy Hour, driving either a fast, foreign car or a big America truck on the commute to work, and counting his accruing money at all hours.

He's always dressed in perfect coordination, whether it's a Ralph Lauren suit complemented with a purple tie, or sporting Gucci loafers with a t-shirt and jeans, and, with the exception of the office, where the pressure to earn more, more, more never ends, or when his latest, greatest cell phone slash e-mailer slash music device slash address book slash microwave oven quits working. He is generally a nice guy, if for no other reason than he was taught by his congenial, homespun parents to be that way. And he's got hobbies, too. Man, does he ever have hobbies. There are golf bags filled with the biggest of the big, bad drivers and the hottest new irons and a putter designed by former NASA engineers. There are shotguns and rifles, decks of cards, boats, skis—for water and snow—bows and arrows, yesterday's sports pages, tomorrow's sports pages, and televisions everywhere. And topping it all off is his signature possession: that metal contraption that truly stokes the wood chips of his heart, relaxing him with its zesty mesquite incense—yes, I'm talking about that instrument of redneckosexual nirvana—the meat-smoker slash barbecue grill.

Any upwardly mobile, married, thirty-something Southern male, knowing the difference between *Men's Journal* and *Sports Illustrated* and worth his salt, owns at least one, and it's likely a favorite source of both pride and those rare-but-precious idle moments. A kind of kiss-my-butt-honey-I-can't-do-chores-around-the-house-for-once-today-because-as-you-see-I'm-cooking-somethin'-on-the-grill-for-the-entire-mother-fucking-family type of hobby with strong psychological roots reaching back to the days when man hunted, literally, for all bestial foods that the family would then barbecue over their campfire slash smoker.

In other words, it serves as an excuse to relieve men of the seemingly more feminine chores of life, like changing sheets or picking up toys around the house on a Saturday morning. But it also serves as a kind of exoneration from some of the questionably feminine preferences of lifestyle these same men enjoy, like hair permanents, spa days, and manicures. The metrosexual has a non-gendered purse; the redneckosexual has his heavily-gendered smoker slash grill, and he's not afraid to use it.

The appliance of choice for the fortunate and the more informed is the big, oblong-shaped ceramic shell known as "A Big Green Egg." This smoker slash grill is revered by men-who-know throughout the South. They trade secrets of recipes and their expert understanding of the apparatus from office to office, from corporation to corporation, and from supper club to supper club. When secretaries or wives see them cloistered in the corner, strutting in front of one another in that swagger of haberdashery, talking from the sides of their mouths and laughing while F-bombs drop like it's Pearl Harbor all over again, they might suspect the men are whispering tales of escapades with wild women, but in all likelihood, the boys are talking about how long they smoked their hens on Saturday.

"Man," says one of the guys-who-know, "I got that bitch too hot. She was tipping off at seven hundred degrees, so, you know, I had to bring her on down, man. I eased that bitch on back to about 300, then, you know, I slid my chicken on in. In about four hours, my fucking bird was right, man. I mean right."

In my larger-than-life family, we are fortunate to have two redneckosexuals by virtue of marriage—JT and Frank, two of Atlanta's finest financial product brokers. Without question, the boys, as I call them, are the life of the group at gatherings and ever a source of my amusement. And without question, what they talk about more than anything else is their beloved smoker slash grills and what they've barbecued most recently and what gadgets they've acquired to make their grueling job easier.

For example, I recall one recent Thanksgiving, when I accidentally became cornered by the boys when they were well past a few beers and a couple glasses of wine each. We were at JT's swanky lake house somewhere in Georgia. He was pointing to the water, explaining how, with his new thermometer, he could actually get updated readings from his smoker slash grill while riding in his boat and pulling his precious little children on skis.

"That's some shit right there, isn't it?"

And it was.

Because the boys are so adored by the family and

because their passions impel them to take such action into their own hands, a few years ago we began to allow them to take over the big job of preparing the turkeys for family holiday gatherings. This is no small job, considering that often 35 or more relatives show up, expecting to be well fed. It is one thing to be responsible for bringing, say, wine. Just grab a handful of moderately priced bottles of anything red and rest assured that by mid-afternoon it'll all be gone. The same can be said for mashed potatoes, broccoli casserole, and gravy; I've yet to see any go to waste. But turkeys are a different deal because for many years we had an excellent cook who reliably kept the family well fed before passing on and leaving us in need. The boys volunteered, and what were we to say?

The first year they were in charge, the turkeys came out okay, but the same couldn't be said for JT's car. With a big new SUV in the driveway—back in the day when having a big new SUV in the driveway was cool—JT was looking for a place to store his freshly cooked turkeys for the night. He only had two breasts because it was to be a smaller-than-average gathering, but they were cooked the night before in hope of avoiding any first-time mistakes. With the breasts completely done by 11 p.m. and lunch some 13 hours away, he was off to a good start. But because the birds were too large to fit into the refrigerator, he needed a place to store them.

Considering that the forecast called for the temperature to be down in the forties overnight, the rooftop of the SUV seemed like a logical solution. The turkeys would be refrigerated by nature and kept out of reach of his two gifted Labrador retrievers. He had guessed correctly that the dogs couldn't reach the top of the car, but Mr. Redneckosexual failed to consider that the dogs might at least *try to get* the bird breasts.

Arriving the next morning, I couldn't help but notice that nearly all the paint had been scratched from the doors of both the driver's and passenger's side of the cool new SUV. In trying to reach the breasts, the dogs must have leapt one hundred times each toward the top, raking their claws back down the car every time.

"Guess I had better wait till morning to cook them next time," JT said.

Because the crowd had anticipated the family gathering, the next year was three times as large. And because JT didn't want to disappoint, he enlisted the help of Frank, his brother-in-law, who lived around the corner and who also had a smoker slash grill. The plan was that, in order to have enough bird for almost 40 guests, one person would cook two breasts, while the other would cook one extremely large whole bird. With experience in hand, JT took responsibility for the breasts, advising Frank that he needn't start his big turkey until early in the morning the day of the event.

Shortly after lunch, JT arrived with his breasts—enough to feed one-third of the gathered crowd. One hour later, Frank arrived, urging the hostess to crank up her oven. Before it was even preheated, he plunged the bird in, wiping November sweat from his brow after the door closed.

"Give it an hour," he said.

"An hour!" I wanted to scream, "Have you any idea how hungry these people are?"

An hour and a half later, we had to carve the bird or starve the guests. For more than 20 minutes, Frank poked and prodded, searching for edible meat. The result was several large piles of finely chopped bird, akin to chopped pork at your favorite barbecue dive. The crowd ate, appreciative of the effort, and it was not until later in the day, when a first-time guest inquired if we "always chopped our turkey that way," that we realized how botched the bird had been.

Hoping that experience would prevail, and not wanting to trample the boys' hearts by insulting their pride and joy, we let them attempt the birds yet another time. The following year, with the gathering slated for his house, JT, with the assistance of Frank, was back on the job. Arriving early in the morning, I watched them work together, injecting some sort of flavored goop into the big turkey with the precision of a skilled surgeon. Then I watched them tend to the coveted smoker slash grill. Clad in Gucci loafers and designer jeans, they poked and prodded the fire to perfection. Then the turkey was placed inside and the valves closed down in an effort to get the temperature just right. The lid was never opened, but throughout the day the grill was watched steadily. I tried talking during this ritual, but found the boys only half-listening, if at all.

"How's your baby girl?"

"What's that?" Frank responded. "Oh, great, great,

man—look, she's just smoking along. That temperature is holding tight."

"How's work?"

"It seems to be working okay," JT said, "but we might need to add some wood chips."

But lo and behold, at 4:30 in the afternoon one turkey, bronzed to perfection in the smoker slash grill, was brought inside the house. Thirty minutes later, it was carved and served and, to a person, it was loved. No comments about chopped bird, no sweat dripping from the brow, just the taste of succulent turkey.

This is not to suggest that these meat-smoking sons of guns had mastered their greatest challenge, holiday meat; it is simply giving credit where credit is due. I will admit, however, that the glory was short lived, considering that the very next year, JT overslept due to a bout with the cocktail flu and did not get the turkey onto the smoker slash grill until almost nine in the morning, making it a full three hours late for the Thanksgiving party. And it is true that in an effort to get the bird done faster, he ignored rule number one, passed along from one redneckosexual to another in a singsong manner and belted out to the tune of a popular Foghat rock song: *cook all meat slow and easy…*

The bird was so charred when JT brought it in to an empty table that it appeared more like a relic abandoned in a house fire than something suitable for dinner. Standing nearby, Frank was so flustered that he was at a rare loss for words—unable, even, to utter a smartass remark. I could have sworn, in fact, that I saw what might have been a tear dribbling down his too-thin cheek. Turning away, I looked squarely at JT, who was struggling to hold the super-large, belatedly done turkey on a platter. I could see the pain on his well-moisturized face, the furrowing of his neatly plucked brows.

"Relax," I told him. "Christmas is just around the corner. Just refrigerate that thing on top of your car until then, and for a change you'll be a step ahead for the next gathering."

The Metrosexual vs. The Redneckosexual

Metrosexual

1. Chases sushi dinner with small scoop of mango sorbet served by the waiter.
2. Goes to salon for pubic-area wax job.
3. Carries a leather bag.
4. Has a cat which purrs.
5. Drives a small, precision car.
6. Reads magazines on the weekend.
7. Refused to look at Britney Spears no-underwear photos on the internet.
8. Eats tempeh, knows it comes from beans.
9. Was a cheerleader at Boston University.
10. Owns Earl jeans.

Redneckosexual

1. Chases sushi dinner with giant sized Reese's Peanut Butter Cups bought at convenience store on way home.
2. Goes to salon for traditional haircut and bold enough to ask for eyebrow trim.
3. Has an affair with a leather bag.
4. Has a Labrador which fetches.
5. Drives a big, bulky truck.
6. Fires up a smoker slash grill on the weekend.
7. Emails Britney Spears no-underwear photos on the internet to friends.
8. Eats tempeh, thinks it comes from cows.
9. Dated a cheerleader at Auburn University.
10. Owns jeans; named Earl.

I'm Not Leaving Until I Eat This Thing

John T. Edge

It's just past four on a Thursday afternoon in June at Jesse's Place, a country juke thirty-five miles south of the Mississippi line, three miles west of Amite, Louisiana. The air conditioner hacks and spits forth torrents of arctic air, but the heat of summer can't be kept at bay. It seeps around the splintered door jambs and settles in, transforming the squat, particle-board plastered roadhouse into a sauna. Slowly, the dank barroom fills with grease-smeared mechanics from the truck stop up the road and farmers straight from the fields, the soles of their brogans thick with dirt clods. A few weary souls make their way over from the nearby sawmill, the kind of place where more than one worker has muscled a log into the chipper and drawn back a nub.

I sit alone at the bar, one empty bottle of Bud in front of me, a second in my hand. I drain the beer, order a third, and stare down at the pink juice spreading outward from a crumpled foil pouch, across the paper towel that serves as my makeshift placemat, and onto the dull, black vinyl bar.

I'm not leaving until I eat this thing, I tell myself.

*

Half a mile down the road, behind a fence coiled with razor wire, Lionel Dufour, proprietor of Farm Fresh Food Supplier, loads up the last truck of the day, wheeling case after case of pickled pork offal out of his cinderblock processing plant and into a semi-trailer bound for Hattiesburg, Mississippi.

His crew packed lips today. Yesterday it was pickled sausage, the day before that, pig feet. Tomorrow, it's pickled pig lips again. And today, like every other weekday, Lionel has been on the job since a quarter 'til three in the morning, when he came in to light the boilers. Damon Landry, chief cook and maintenance man, came in at four-thirty. By seven-thirty, the production line was at full tilt: six women in white smocks and blue bouffant caps, slicing ragged white fat from the lips, tossing the good parts in glass jars, the bad parts in barrels bound for the rendering plant. Across the aisle, filled jars clatter by on a conveyor belt as a worker tops them off with a Kool-Aid-red slurry of hot sauce, vinegar, salt, and food coloring. Around the corner, the jars are capped, affixed with a label, and stored in pasteboard boxes to await shipping.

Unlike most offal, lips belie their provenance. Brains, milky white and globular, look like brains; feet, the ghosts of their cloven hoofs protruding, look like feet; and testicles look like, well, testicles. But lips are different. Loosed from the snout, trimmed of their fat, and dyed a preternatural pink, they look more like candy than carrion.

At Farm Fresh, no swine root in an adjacent feedlot. No viscera-strewn killing floor lurks just out of sight, down a darkened hallway. These pigs died long ago at some Midwestern abattoir. No trace remains of their trauma. By the time the lips arrive in Amite, they are, in essence, pig Popsicles, fifty-pound blocks of offal and ice.

"Lips are all meat," Lionel told me earlier in the day. "No gristle, no bone, no nothing. They're bar food, hot and vinegary, great with a beer. Used to be the lips ended up in sausages, headcheese, those sorts of things. A lot of them still do."

Lionel, a fifty-year-old father of three with quick, intelligent eyes set deep in a face the color of cordovan, is a veteran of nearly forty years in the pickled pig lip business. "I started out with my daddy when I wasn't much more than ten," Lionel told me, his shy smile framed by a coarse black mustache flecked with whispers of gray. "The meat-packing business he owned had gone broke back when I was six, and he was peddling out of the back of his car, selling dried shrimp, BC powders, napkins, straws, tubes of plastic cups, pig feet, pig lips, whatever the bar owners needed. He sold to black bars, white bars, sweet shops, snow ball stands; you name it. We made the rounds together after I got out of school, sometimes staying out 'til two or three in the morning. I remember bringing my toy cars to this one joint and racing them around the floor with the bar owner's son while my daddy and his father did business."

For years after the demise of that first meat-packing

company, the Dufour family sold someone else's product, someone else's lips. "We used to buy lips from Dennis Di Salvo's company down in Belle Chasse," recalled Lionel. "As far as I can tell, his mother was the one who came up with the idea to pickle and pack lips back in the 50s, back when she was working for a company called Three Little Pigs over in Houma. But pretty soon, we were selling so many lips that we had to almost beg the Di Salvos for product. That's when we started cooking up our own," he told me, gesturing toward the cast-iron kettle that hangs from the rafters by the front door. "My daddy started cooking lips in that very pot."

Lionel now cooks his lips in seven retrofitted milk tanks, dull stainless-steel caldrons shaped like oversized cradles. But little else has changed about the business. Though his father has passed away, Farm Fresh remains a family-focused company. His wife, Kathy, keeps the books. His daughter, Dana, a button-cute college student who has won numerous beauty titles, takes to the road in the summer, selling lips to convenience stores and wholesalers. Soon, after he graduates from business school, Lionel's youngest son, Matt, will take over operations at the plant. And his oldest son, a veterinarian, lent his name to one of Farm Fresh's trademark items, Jason's Pickled Pig Lips.

"We do our best to corner the market on lips," Lionel told me, his voice tinged with not a little bravado. "Sometimes they're hard to get from the packing houses. You gotta kill a lot of pigs to get enough lips to keep us going. I've got new customers calling every day; it's all I can do to keep up with demand, but I bust my ass to keep up. I do what I can for my family—and for my customers.

"When my customers tell me something," he continued, "just like when my daddy told me something—I listen. If my customers wanted me to dye the lips green, I'd ask, 'What shade?' As it is, every few years we'll do some red and some blue for the Fourth of July. This year we did jars full of Mardi Gras lips—half purple, half gold," Lionel recalled with a chuckle. "I guess we'd had a few beers when we came up with that one."

*

Meanwhile, back at Jesse's Place, I finish my third Bud, order my fourth. *Now*, I tell myself, my courage bolstered by booze, *I'm ready to eat a lip*.

They may have looked like candy in the plant, but in the barroom they're carrion once again. I poke and prod the six-inch arc of pink flesh, peering up from my reverie just in time to catch the barkeep's wife, Audrey, staring straight at me. She fixes me with a look just this side of pity and, as I continue to toy with the lip, wonders aloud, "You gonna eat that thing or make love to it?"

Her nephew, Jerry, sidles up to a barstool on my left. "A lot of people like 'em with chips," he says with a nod of the head toward the pink juice pooling on the bar in front of me. I offer to buy him a lip and Audrey fishes it from a jar back behind the counter, wraps it in tinfoil, and places the whole affair on a paper towel in front of him.

I take stock of my own culinary cowardice, and, following Jerry's lead, reach for a bag of potato chips, tear open the top with my teeth, and toss the quivering hunk of hog flesh into the shiny interior of the bag, slick with grease and dusted with salt. Vinegar vapors tickle my nostrils. I stifle a gag that seems to roll from the back of my throat, swallow hard, and pray that the urge to vomit passes. It does.

With a smash of my hand, the potato chips are reduced to a pulp, and I feel the cold lump of the lip beneath my fist. I clasp the bag shut, shaking it hard in an effort to ensure chip coverage in all the nooks and crannies of the lip. The technique Jerry uses—and I mimic—is not unlike that employed by homemakers mixing up a mess of Shake 'n Bake chicken.

I pull the lip from the bag, a coral crescent of meat now crusted with blond bits of potato chips. When I chomp down, the soft flesh dissolves between my teeth. It tastes like a flaccid cracklin', unmistakably porcine, and not altogether bad. The chips help, providing texture where there was none. My brow unfurrows, my stomach ceases its fluttering.

Sensing my relief, Jerry leans over and peers into my bag. "Kind of look like Frosted Flakes, don't they?" he says, by way of describing the chips rapidly turning to mush upon contact with the pickling juice. I offer the bag to Jerry, order yet another beer, and turn to eye the pig feet floating in a murky jar by the cash register, their blunt tips bobbing up through a pasty white film.

Man Showers, Faux Fireplaces, and a Doorbell That Chimes the Theme from Rhinestone Cowboy

Lisa Daily

"We're buying the ugly house," I informed my husband tearfully as I followed the real estate agent back to her office.

My husband was inconveniently (for me, lucky for him) stuck at a conference in Washington, DC, in a convention center with sketchy cell phone reception. And I, six months pregnant and toting our cranky three-year-old, was speed-shopping for real estate.

"What's the difference if I'm there or not?" he joked. "You're just going to talk me into buying the one you like anyway. Why not eliminate the middleman?"

He had a point.

My husband had been promoted, and our family was being relocated. Or maybe, dislocated. I had just two short days to find our new home. And I was dragging our potty-training-in-progress toddler along for the ride.

After several years of living in the frozen North, we were finally moving back to the South, and buying our very first home. Granted, I'd been hoping for Charleston or Richmond, but South Florida was as close as we could get. (Yes, I realize there are many in the world who do not consider Florida to be a part of the South, but frankly, they had sweet tea and warm weather. This was a corporate relocation, and I was going to have to take what I could get.)

Hacking the ice off my windshield for five months out of the year was not the reason I needed to get back to the South. Much of my family hails from the South; Southerners are my people. My family recipes all contain a large measure of grease and sugar, I yearned for the scent of magnolias, I wanted my children to grow up speaking with the melodic lilt of the South. I wanted to live in a place where strangers at the grocery store would reinforce the good manners I was teaching at home, would insist that my young son refer to them as *ma'am* or *sir*, and would never, as has happened on many occasions in the North, say to a toddler, "Just call me Jim."

Day one did not start off well. Our real estate agent was recommended to us by my husband's company: her sole qualification, I later learned, was the willingness to kick back some of her commission to the relocation company.

Being the domestically inclined, hyper-organized, researching lunatic that I am, I'd been scouring the online real estate listings for weeks. When I spoke with our assigned agent on the phone the week before we were set to arrive in Florida, I told her I had three requirements:

1. We wanted a buyers' agent (someone who only represents buyers, not sellers).
2. I wanted to see the houses I'd faxed over in the exact order I'd specified.
3. I did not want to see the ugly banana-yellow house that fit our every requirement, yet was so aesthetically horrific that no sane person could possibly reside there.

I'm not the kind of person who needs to see 43 houses in order to realize the first one was perfect. I am the kind of person, however, who likes her directives to be followed.

In the real estate world, my husband and I were a slam dunk. We needed to purchase a house immediately because we were moving in three weeks. We had a nice-sized deposit at the ready and a pre-approval letter in hand. We were every lazy real estate agent's fantasy come true: One, maybe two days of work, and a nice fat commission check.

When my son and I met with the agent on day one, she informed us that she was indeed a buyer's agent. Unless, of course, we happened to decide that we wanted to buy one of her company's listings, and then she would magically morph into what they liked to call a "dual agent." Dual agent, as in representing both the buyer *and* the seller. I was not happy. I thought I'd made it pretty clear that a "dual agent" was the very thing I was trying to avoid. She smiled a squinty little smile and ran her fingers through the ragged ends of her bleached-blonde hair. But she knew, and

I knew, that I was stuck with her. I had to find a house by tomorrow.

We set off in the direction of potential house number one, stopping off first at a three-bedroom shack with a frog-green pool and carpet that smelled like a retirement home for Great Danes. The house was more than a hundred thousand dollars below our target price. It was not on my list.

When we pulled into the driveway, the owner of said shack was chain smoking in the driveway. I was almost positive I'd seen her on *Jerry Springer*. Or maybe she was the yodeling knife juggler on *America's Got Talent*. My first instinct was to slam the rental car in reverse, peel out of the neighborhood, and leave the "dual agent" to fend for herself, but the owner sprinted over to my door and rapped her knuckles on the window. My good manners kicked in, and I forced myself to at least tour the house. I got out of the car slowly, trying not to make any sudden moves.

"We're gonna get the pool fixed!" she rasped in a voice that sounded like a bad-girl Phyllis Diller, the cigarette dangling from her lip.

As we stepped through the front door, I held my son close to me and tried not to inhale. Three minutes later we were back at our cars, four minutes later we were having a pow-wow in the parking lot at the Piggly Wiggly.

"I don't want to see any more crack dens," I told her.

"I thought maybe..." she stammered.

"Please," I said. "Just take me to the houses on my list. At least four bedrooms, no more than $20,000 above or below the number I told you."

Lesson number one in real estate school is to show the buyers all of the crappy houses first, so that by the time they see the good house, they'll feel like they've stumbled on Shangri-la. "I know about the crack-house-to-palace model," I said. "Just take me to the good stuff. I can barely fit behind the steering wheel, I have to stop to pee every five minutes, my son is already beginning to howl, and one more chocolate-covered bribe is going send the kid into a sugar coma."

Two inappropriate houses later, our real estate agent was ready to pack it in for the day. It was lunchtime, and I still hadn't seen any of the houses on my list.

"I have to find a house by tomorrow!" I said.

"We'll get an early start," she promised.

I loaded my son back into his car seat and headed to the hotel, leaving a message for the dual agent that we would no longer be needing her services. I now had one day to find a house. And no agent.

Back at the hotel, I called the listing agent for house number one on my list. I ended up telling her my entire story, bawling my eyes out to this complete stranger.

"There, there," she soothed, "we'll find your house tomorrow." She promised to clear her entire schedule for the next day, show me any houses I'd like in the exact order I specified. She even offered to send her mother over to scout a new possibility that had popped up just that morning, one that was not on my list. This was a woman who understood an easy commission when she saw one.

The next morning we started off, list in hand. The nice agent had brought her mother along, also a real estate agent, who attempted to entertain my child as we rushed through the homes of strangers. I eliminated the houses one by one: This neighborhood isn't what I was hoping for. This house appears to have been built for the seven dwarves. This one has no storage. (And, um, an alligator in the backyard.)

By four-thirty in the afternoon on my last day, I was desperate and at the end of my list. I told the nice agent and her mother that I wanted to do the unthinkable: I wanted to see the ugly yellow house.

The ugly yellow house sat on a quiet cul-de-sac, a block away from the best elementary school in the district. It had four bedrooms and an office, Mexican ceramic tile and a stunning banana palm providing shade for the resort-style pool. It also had forest-green carpet paired with a turquoise hallway, a peach-and-navy blue living room, and a murder-red guest room with weird Rob and Laura Petrie single-bed built-ins made of government-issue beige laminate.

Each room in the house was papered in an abundant selection of the most hideous old-lady wallpapers money can buy, complete with one, sometimes two coordinating borders. The kitchen, which boasted the stunning Mexican ceramic tile, also featured orange laminate counters that ran all the way up the wall, all the way up to the faux-est faux wood cabinets I'd ever seen. And the half-wall in the formal living room had synthetic green marble insets to coordinate with the fake fireplace. Fake fireplace. As in, not an actual fireplace. Just a mantel and a hearth glued to the wall, complete with a collection of plastic logs that kind of glowed when you plugged them into the wall socket.

And there was no bathtub. Instead, the very large master bath had what we later dubbed "the man shower." It was a huge, tiled room overlooking a toilet. Like a locker room, but with only one showerhead. And no hot water.

The owners claimed to be two gay men, but I think they must have been fronting. Stereotype or not, every gay man I'd ever met in my life had exquisite taste; these guys just had to be posers.

The bones of the house were wonderful, classic, quality. But it was nearly impossible to see beyond the tacky wall coverings, haunted-house-style shrubbery, and the owners' obvious passion for laminate.

The house was a tarted-up classic—like a Vanderbilt—decked out in frosted pink lipstick, a spandex miniskirt, and a sparkly boob tube straight from the clearance rack at Wal-Mart.

In the end, we bought the ugly yellow house, which we dubbed "the Banana Palace." It was our first house. It was big. The neighborhood was great. And we figured we could temporarily live with the fact that we owned the ugliest house in the state. We stripped out the horrid green carpet, painted everything in sight, hacked down the jungle in front of the house, invested in a professional-grade wallpaper steamer, and hired a team of cleaning ladies to scour the place from top to bottom. A year later, the house was unrecognizable. It was our home.

The miracle of the Banana Palace is how it brought our family together. My husband and I hung light fixtures together. My mother and my aunts flew in to help us paint, strip wallpaper, and demolish the electric fireplace. Our son peeled off wallpaper as high as he could reach and learned how to use a paint roller. In the beginning, it seemed every day revealed a new problem, or something else that had been neglected by the former owners. But in the process of peeling and painting and refurbishing, our family grew closer. We giggled together about the man shower and the fake fireplace, and the fact that our doorbell chimed the theme from *Rhinestone Cowboy*.

And that old house, which started out as the house we settled for, became the home we loved.

In Cold Mud

Jim Dees

My fishing buddy Skip Zanzibar will pull off his shirt during most any angling outing, and if it's hot enough, and we stay out long enough, his pants will drop like an anchor. Skip's a big boy—he says he weighs "a eighth of a ton." I've never bothered to do the math, but I think it's close to three hundred pounds. Seeing him naked is tough duty, compounded by the fact that his skin is a work-in-distress. His "bark," as he calls it, is a ruddy, quilt patchwork of skin grafts owing to a burning accident in infancy: a gas heater exploded next to his crib.

Skip grew up scalded and screaming, so I suppose it's no wonder he rather enjoys doffing his duds now and again, particularly when there is cold water at hand and the fish don't appear to be using it. On our forays, I would leave Skip to his nakedness as I never much cared for fishing in the buff. There's nowhere to put your wallet. Plus, fishing involves the flight of hooks through the air, a fact rife with scenarios I'm not prepared to trifle with.

We fished various sloughs on the backwaters of the Tallahatchie River, and all were a good distance from the nearest road, accessible only by the hearty or drunk. These trips required trampling through thickets, a marsh that welled up in your sneakers like Jell-O, and over two hills, until one reached the series of sloughs filled with fish and water from the spring rains. One could damn near work up a half-decent hallucination on these long, difficult walks to the water. Skip and I liked to mix a little Zen into the experience by attempting to visualize the fish; where they were and why.

Such reveries were, shall we say, "punctuated" when Skip put down his gear, and owing to a twenty-year cigarette habit, coughed up a sludge of what appeared to be roofing tar. The walk was strenuous enough, but of course we humped it with full gear: a packed ice chest, two triple-racked tackle boxes, six rods for the two of us, and Skip's two-way radio to monitor the Cubs game.

On arrival, we would split up and walk separately among the various sandy craters. Often I would see him far in the distance, wading into the lake naked, all round, white, and pockmarked, like the moon going in for a bath.

There was nothing skinny about his dipping.

On one particular trip, we were joined by our buddy Truck, who may be the perfect fishing companion because he talks even less than fish. We pulled up in his driveway in the predawn hours, and he slipped into the truck, saying,

"Mornin'," and that was it until noon. During the long ride to the fishing hole, Truck sipped his breakfast beer and stared out the window, noting flora and fowl. Truck and I were lost, but Skip knew these back roads and backwaters from childhood. He had grown up in North Mississippi and then moved away, drifting down to the Gulf Coast to ply the waters as a boatman. He returned often to Lafayette County to visit his aged mother and casserole corps of great aunts, and on these sojourns, much like an ancient bass, he would return to his haunts.

Skip was always nonplussed when coming across barbed wire on the trail. It ultimately meant bending low while Truck and I pulled the wire up with all our muster. Skip concentrated on sucking in his gut—which was roughly the size and shape of a Volkswagen Beetle—and shimmying through the opening we'd made. All of this while trying not to catch his Hawaiian print shorts on the barbs, lose his cigarette, or spill his beer. Somehow, gravity was thwarted and Skip made it. We took it as a sign. We figured if his gut had made it through, and he didn't cut his shriveled skin, rip his surfer shorts, or spill his Natural Light, the fishing gods might just have a sense of humor.

This theory bore fruit on this day. We were actually catching fish when the new owner (the barbed fence should have been a tip-off) suddenly walked out of the woods and demanded to know "What the F are you doing?" and "Just how long do you think it will take you to get your F-ing butts out of here?" He really said "F" and "F-ing," screeching in a twangy singsong like Barney Fife on helium.

"This is private property," he warned us, "and y'all need to get on the F word out of here. I'm trying to quit cussing for my wife—but y'all need to git."

Truck and I looked at each other and quickly set to gathering everything up. The little man was drawn up into a small frame of contempt. His grimy overalls hung loose, and his hands were gnarled and tan—not from fishing, I suspected, but from milking cows, feeding pigs, and hoeing greens. He had the determined, beady-eyed look of someone who easily reverted to his most craven instincts.

"We didn't mean no harm," Truck said, reeling in his line and pulling in our mesh bucket, which held about six nice crappie.

"You can just put them fish back, too." The man tightened his jaw and reached his hand into his pocket.

Truck and I quickly gathered our stuff while keeping a close eye on the little country terrorist. We gasped as he pulled an object out of his pocket. It turned out to be a cell phone.

"Y'all want me to call the sheriff?"

Truck emptied the fish back into the water and collapsed the bucket.

"Let me holler for ol' Skip, and we're out of here. We sure are sorry, we didn't know—"

"Holler for who? You mean y'all got a third one out there?" The man looked even beadier as he squinted at the shimmering distance. He started walking toward the tree where Skip's clothes hung. We followed and started to make lame conversation to distract him.

"I'm sorry, sir, but I didn't catch your name. My name

is Truck, and this here is Jim Dees, and our friend Skip is out here. I'm sorry, mister? Uh, mister, I didn't..."

The man stared back at Truck with a blank face such as the best poker players employ.

"I am *Tiger Woods*," he twanged and kept walking.

Truck and I looked at each other and shook our heads. The three of us walked to the water's edge, where Skip's clothes were hanging and their flapping matched the water's sounds, lapping at the bank. Then, with a loud *swoosh!!* Skip rose up out of the water, rod and reel in hand, wearing nothing but mud and indignation. Skip is a big man, and he appeared to be fighting a truly big fish. Tiger Woods was not very happy and who could blame him? Not only was he dealing with trespassers and fish thieves, but he was also being confronted with the visual jolt of Skip in all his gnarly, crispy splendor.

"What the H is it?" Tiger Woods asked, eyeballing more acreage of ruined human flesh than he'd ever hoped not to see on a single man.

"That's ol' Skip," Truck said brightly. He called out, "Skip, this here is Mr. Tiger Woods."

"Pleased to meetcha, Mr. Woods," Skip said, with one eye on his quivering rod. He was about 15 yards out and treading water, letting the giant fish circle, hoping to tire him before attempting to reel him in. "I'll be with you in a minute, Mr. Tiger. I think this is a 30-pound catfish, don't know if I'll ever get him up."

"Skip, huh?" spat the man who gave his name as Tiger

Woods. "Well you fat, naked jaybird, I'd hate to pay your grocery bill. Good Lordy, son, there's two ends to a fork, you know. You ought to try setting one down sometime.

"Look here, you just can just *skip* your merry A off of my property and leave that catfish where he lay. That's my catfish, my water, and this here is my enforcement."

We looked over, and Woods had pulled a derringer from his boot. The fish dragged Skip another five feet out into the water. Now he was up to his neck in, among other things, muddy water.

Despite the present trouble, my Zen kicked in. I tried to visualize what Skip must have looked like to the fish in the slough. Here was an eighth of a ton of bulk human flesh, splashing and bobbing like a tasered rhino. What did the little bream think? A cow had cannonballed into the water?

"Now hold on there," Truck said, raising his hands. "There ain't no call for all that. We're leaving, and we'll behave while we do it. We ain't from around here, but we'll act right. Come on out of there, Skip! Just cut the line and leave that catfish and Mr. Woods be. It's time to go."

Skip looked back at Truck with a foul grimace. As he turned his head for the first time, we could see the soggy cigarette lodged behind his ear. We knew he would microwave it and smoke it later.

"Et tu, Truckie?" Skip hissed before being pulled completely under water. The slough roiled and erupted for a moment and then only chocolate bubbles disturbed the surface. Truck and I and the man who called himself Tiger Woods watched the spot a full ten seconds. We kept thinking Skip would bob to the top, but there was no sign of him or the catfish.

"I reckon he can stay under there till the turtles chew off his pee-pee," Tiger Woods said, spitting. "I don't give a good rat's A." His face darkened even more. *Whoosh!!* Skip came up spitting water and shaking his hair, holding the rod with one hand and treading water with the other.

"He's 'bout got a ass on him, don't he?" Skip puffed, shooting us a quick glance. "Y'all want me to get him up?"

"Son, just swim on in here, cut your line, and y'all get off this property," Tiger commanded. "Y'all are trespassing, and I damn sure don't mind acting in self-*dee*fense." Hearing the word "damn" caused Truck and me to look up.

"Okay, one D bit!"

"Sir, this appears to be a fish of some significant proportions," Skip said, gasping above the water. "We need to at least look at him."

"Son, do I need to remind you that I am holding a loaded gun, and you ain't exactly a small target?"

"No sir, you got that pea shooter, and I got a 30-pound catfish," Skip said. "Right now I think God is with me. Frankly sir, no offense intended." Truck and I shook our heads. "But I feel the presence of something bigger and more powerful than us...more powerful than men or fish or even bullets."

Tiger Woods leveled the derringer at Skip.

"Son, for the last time—"

"You can shoot, but when they find me they'll know I was unarmed. Who'd shoot a naked man?"

"Why, a man with the sense to be dressed and holding a firearm on a nudie trespasser, that's who," Woods said.

Truck and I knew what we had to do, and we did it. We took off our clothes.

Woods wheeled around.

"I'd damn, no wonder you boys is single."

At that moment, Skip surfaced, blowing water and struggling with what appeared to be the tire off an 18-wheeler. After he and the fish rolled another couple of times, we saw it was more like a 75-pound flathead catfish that was nearly as long as Skip. Skip had run the stringer through the giant snout of the behemoth and then tied the rope around his wrist and dragged the fish up from the bottom. He carefully led his prey like a sheriff doing the perp walk.

"Yeah, bring that fish on in here," Woods said, even though it was obvious Skip was doing just that. We all gathered at the water's edge, watching Skip grapple with his quarry. We approached and I suppose it was the biggest catfish I had ever seen—70-something pounds. Almost six feet long, its head the size of a scoop shovel, greased with mud, its face seized in exhausted terror, its mouth a foot around displaying a truly epic row of tiny teeth that guarded the deep dark gullet that could easily slurp down a dog or a small child.

The naked, damaged Skip turned to face us muddied, bloodied, and crippled.

"Would you look at the size of that thing?" Truck said, and I think we all knew he was referring to the fish. "Now you can just put him back, mister. Let him go before he dies," Tiger

Woods said, gesturing with the pistol. "Turn him out, fat boy! Turn him out," Tiger screamed, and as he did, he accidentally let the pistol fly, which one-hopped perfectly into the colossal catfish's gaping mouth. Skip poked the giant fish once, and it darted under water.

We all stood there, three of us naked, as the last splash from the beast's tail subsided, and the only sound was the wind and Skip's wheeze. Tiger Woods stood looking at his empty hand while Truck and I exhaled sweaty relief. Skip put his hands on his love handles, which were more like shelves.

"I never knew catch and release meant my heart," he said.

*

By the time we reached Skip's sky blue 1966 Cadillac, the twilight was building around a full moon. The horizon and trees were bathed in a tantalizing blue—everything blue except the lightning bugs. We carefully stored our gear in the massive trunk, where Skip also kept many scavenged items including bowling balls, a knife collection, and a wedding dress still in the box. The full moon had crested and rode the treeline like a surfer when Skip pulled the old Cadillac out onto the road. Once we got going, he let down the top and put in a CD of Fats Waller's "The Jitterbug Waltz," by Rashon Roland Kirk.

"If y'all want to go fishing tomorrow, I know a place," Skip said, popping a Budweiser.

Truck looked at me.

"You up for it?"

"I wouldn't be nuts if I said no," I answered.

I looked over at Skip. He had cut off the headlights, and the road ahead glistened like a snake, and he was gliding the Big Caddy by the cool light of the moon. He had also taken off his shirt and flung it heavenward. The Cadillac rolled on, loaded with tackle and knives and matrimony wear, and ready to deliver us to our next fishing mystery. Truck and I popped beers and that first bracing gulp felt like a just reward. I looked back in time to see Skip's shirt, billowing like a sail as it floated on up toward the moon, naked and free, like a 70-pound catfish.

SALLY THE SCREAMER

ED WILLIAMS

A good love story just can't be beat. I know that for a fact. Since I lucked out with my first book, I've had the pleasure of meeting and getting to know some really fine romance novelists like Rebecca Paisley, Trish Jensen, and Linda Bleser. To be honest, I'd never even read a romance novel prior to meeting these ladies. When I did meet them and discovered what great people they are, I felt that I should read some of their stuff as all of them were nice enough to read my first manuscript.

So I read their books. And I learned plenty. Don't let any of them kid you, either—they know what they're doing. They might look innocently at you and say all this stuff about writing a literary read and all, but don't believe any of it. These ladies write stuff that will make your tongue jump out of your mouth, curl around a tree, and take the bark off it. There is no doubt that stimulation of the libido is a major part of the romance genre. And I think that's great—good writing should make the reader feel *something. And dammit, these ladies have made me feel plenty! They've tented up my britches more times than a duck strains the potatoes.*

After reading their epistles, I started thinking about writing a love story myself. This is pretty much out of character for me, but I thought I'd make a run at it anyway. Writing a good, ol', true-as-it-can-get, Juliette, Georgia, love story. I could even visualize it in my mind—taking some tender story of passion, spinning it in the most romantic way possible, and letting those hot sparks fly.

Finally, I decided to do it. I wrote a Juliettan love story (almost sounds legit, doesn't it?). So get set to buckle up, hunker down (a crumb to all you Georgia fans out there), and read the hauntingly touching account of...Sally the Screamer.

*

"She mooed like a damn cow."

Ed Jr. spouted those loving words as we shared dinner together. The Brotherhood—my two lifelong best friends, Ray Pippin and Hugh Foskey—and Ed Jr., my sixty-eight-year-old dad, breaking bread after a book signing this past Christmas season at the Macon Barnes and Noble.

We were all chewing hot wings at Zaxby's, laughing, and having a good time together after our signing. It was the first and only time we'd all signed books together, and we'd all enjoyed it. It was during this jaw-wearying interlude that I heard one of the most incredibly romantic stories I've ever been made aware of. (I'm fighting back intense emotion at this moment just to get the words down on paper). A story that came straight from the lips of the Godfather, Ed Jr.

The story came up innocently enough. Hugh was discussing a lady at the signing that he felt had the hots for Ed Jr. We all laughed at the thought, as this particular lady had breasts larger than coconuts and a stomach that proportionately matched them. As we ragged out Ed Jr. about her, Ray posed him the $64,000-question, "Could you take care of a woman like that, Godfather?"

Ed Jr. didn't even hesitate. "Let me tell you young spurs something! Take care of her? Hell, y'all would need to hone about ten thousand more tulips each to join the same league that I swing the pink bat in! Y'all just need to sit there, take notes, and listen while I give you a lesson in what being a Williams male really means..."

We were all glued. The old man never broke stride, either.

"E3, when your mom died, I just moped around for a while. Didn't want to do anything and didn't even want to think about being with a woman."

"Time goes by, though, and in my case a couple of years did. I finally got to the point where I was needin' to get my cannon greased pretty badly, if you know what I mean. It's pretty damn pitiful when you start staring and fantasizing about ol' blue-haired women in church that you wouldn't lay on a normal day. That's the point I'd gotten to. Decided that something had to be done, or else I was gonna go crazier than a muddy hen."

At this point, Brother Pippin jumped in and asked the old

man if he wasn't feeding us all a little Aesop? The words had barely gotten out of Brother Pippin's mouth when he got his response.

"I don't have to pretend to like doilies when it comes to women. Hell, a few weeks ago I went down to Juliette and walked into one of the shops to buy my Cash 3 lotto tickets. Turns out an ol' gal from New York was in there looking around. It just so happened that while she was there, her old man was down the street fooling around in another tourist trap. In twenty minutes time I got his old lady into my Jaguar, took her to the house, plowed her like a new crop, and hustled her back so quickly that her husband didn't even know she was gone."

Hugh remarked, "Sounds to me like you had to be pretty fast on the trigger to pull that off."

"Fast—hell," said Ed Jr. "In that case, I had to be. That's another thing you young skeeters need to learn. You have to adapt your honing to the situation you find yourselves in. These Northern women, half of 'em would pass out if you gave 'em a good, down-home, Southern screwing."

You couldn't argue with any of those salient points. At this juncture, we all apologized to Ed Jr. for even beginning to doubt him and asked him to continue his story.

"As I said, I was needing to get laid pretty bad. Finally, one day at the gas plant, Terry Sare came walking up to me. Told me that he had some business to discuss and that we'd best walk outside."

"We went outside, and Terry told me how he had this steady girlfriend named Mable. Said they had been going out for close to two years. I asked him why they hadn't gotten married, and Terry told me he was getting a full drag of milk under the fence, so there was no need to. I could understand that. Anyway, he starts telling me about this woman Mable knows. Said her name was Sally Long. She worked in a bank in Macon and had been widowed herself for several years.

"Terry told me he wanted to fix me up with her, but warned me that I shouldn't expect to have a shot at her britches until at least five or six dates had passed. I told him I understood, and that I was willin' to spend some time with her. Terry smiled and said he'd see what he could do.

"A few days later Terry walks up and tells me that everything has been arranged. That I'm to go over to Sally's house Saturday night along with him and his girlfriend. I asked him what were we all going to do? Terry smiled like he had a mouth full of briars and said that he expected he'd end the evening with his girlfriend in one of the bedrooms, and that Sally and I would probably just sit around, talk, and get better acquainted. I remember thinking that Terry just didn't understand the Williams male, but when you haven't been laid in two years even talkin' to a woman can sound pretty good.

"Finally, Saturday night comes around, and I go on over to Sally's house. I was dressed half-assed decent, and when I got there I found that she had a nice house in one of the better subdivisions in Macon. After scoping out the place for bad dogs and yellow-jacket nests, I knocked on Sally's door and waited.

"Sally came out in a couple of minutes frocked in a nice blue dress. I had to admit that I was a tad disappointed when

I first laid eyes on her. She sure wasn't dressed like anyone who had inclinations toward getting laid. I decided I'd just get to know her and figured that nothing more than a kiss would come out of the evening.

"I was ashamed of myself after thinking that. I'm a Williams male, dammit. Been a line of us Ed Williams ever since the mid-1800s. And the one thing all of us could do well, without exception, was hone the tulip. Hell, I had gone so long without it that I had given up the fight before I'd even gotten inside Sally's house. Then I thought to myself, I may come out of here with my bone dryer than talcum powder, but I'm going to give it my best shot!"

Ray congratulated Ed Jr. on mentally readying himself for success. We all laughed at the Pip, but quieted when Ed Jr. said, "I looked at things the right way, boys."

We all knew this story was about to get a lot more interesting.

"You have to believe that something good is going to happen to you. Half the asses out there give themselves excuses as to why they can't accomplish something. Me? I figure I'm going to do what I want to unless Evander Holyfield is standing between me and my objective. And even he can have his ass whipped by a man that knows how."

At this point, Hugh, Ray, and I were all leaning over in the booth, laughing ferociously. Ed Jr. went on.

"Sally told me to come on inside, and I did. Walked right into her living room, which is where Terry and his girlfriend were. After seeing Mable, I didn't feel so bad about Sally. She was haint ugly, to be blunt with you boys. I've seen better-looking women in chewing tobacco ads. As I drank in her haintness, it hit me as to how some people like Terry will jump in the sack with almost anything that will cooperate.

"Then I tailed Sally out into the kitchen, started talkin', and it turns out Sally is a nice ol' country girl. Grew up in Boxankle, Georgia, so I knew she understood what small-town living was all about. That's important, finding someone from a small town. To tell you the truth, I find a lot of these big-city gals to be like balloons—lots of hot air, but hollow inside. Sally seemed to have her head screwed on pretty straight. She gave the Democrats hell for awhile, and when I mentioned as to how I'd manage the Braves, she basically agreed with me on pretty near everything I said. You have to respect that, that she knew so much about baseball.

"Sally and I kept talking, and I found I really liked her—she was smart, and there wasn't a phony bone in her body. After a few minutes, I decided to go in the living room and see how Terry was doing. I figured with the haint he was dating that he should already have gotten laid and be right close to honin' her tulip again. Ugly women can do that to you, make you ripe to hone 'cause you know you've already flushed your character down the toilet when you screw them.

"When I took a gander in, it was clear to me that Mr. Stud of the Southeast wasn't even getting smiles from Rin Tin Tin. She was sitting in another chair across from Terry lookin' like a stepped-on snake. Seeing that, I figured I would try to be nice and lighten things up. Figured it would be my way of paying Terry back for trying to help me out and all. I smiled at the ugly heifer and mentioned to her how ol' Terry was known at work as a pretty funny guy. Told her that Terry could tell a good joke and all.

"I guess I shouldn't have said that 'cause she shot right back at me. 'I know what you mean,' she said. 'I laugh like hell when he takes his jockey shorts off.'

"Well, Terry started arguing with the haint about the size of his trouser moccasin, and I figured it was a good time to walk back into the kitchen. When I got back in there Sally was laughing like hell. She'd overheard Mable's remark.

"I watched her crack up about Terry having a small tong, and hell, I started laughing again, too. We both laughed so hard that Terry yelled in there and asked us what we were braying about?

"'We're laughing at some of Ed's stories about Korea,' Sally said.

"I had to respect her for that. It was a damn good answer and got the heat off our asses. I triple respected her when she then said, 'Let's go back in my room and relax.'

"Hot damn! I knew what that meant! I was about to get a chance to unlimber the python of pleasure and make my return to the world of tulip honing."

"The world of tulip honing?" Ray spat out part of a hot wing over that one. At this point, Hugh was pleading with Ed Jr. for mercy. There was none given, though. He was on a roll, and continued to freely express himself.

"We walked right back there and shut the door. I noticed that Sally locked it, too. She smiled at me and said that we could watch some TV together. Right after that, she excused herself to go to the bathroom."

"Were you excited, Godfather?" Brother Pippin asked.

"Excited as a pig wallowing in a fresh pile," Ed Jr. responded. "You see, when she went in that bathroom, I knew she wasn't goin' in there for any reason other than she was getting ready to crank up the limo of love. I thought about it for a second and figured it was time to get naked. I mean, I was in her bedroom and all. So I stripped my clothes right off and got in her bed."

We all couldn't believe that he'd just get naked and climb in her bed like that, so I questioned him about it. Ed Jr. got a real serious look going, stared me in the eye, and said, "You have to be kidding! Let me tell you something, boy, that you should always remember. It should be second nature to you, like breathing or watching football.

"No woman invites a Williams male into her bedroom without full well knowing that they're about to do the Dirty Bird of love. It's a given. Hell, my money says that Sally would've been disappointed if I hadn't been naked when she came back in there."

"What did she say when she walked in, ol' man?" I asked.

"Well, she walked back in there in this nice-lookin' nightgown. One of those that you know isn't meant to feed the cat in.

"I was propped up on one arm, and she exhaled loudly when she saw me naked like that. I think, too, that she noticed that my Jimmy Dean was standing up. She looked at it (and me) a long time, and then her eyes got real wide.

"'You're glad to see me,' she said.

"Ma'am, are we here to talk or ride like the wind?"

"After that, things got easy. It wasn't too long before we were pumping like a Jerry Lee Lewis piano. Damn, it was good. So good that I would have even voted a straight Democratic ballot to keep on honing Sally's sweet tulip.

"We were moving like greased eels, having a helluva time, when all of a sudden I heard the funniest sound. It was like... *Mooooooo!*"

Ray, Hugh, and I were close to hospitalization at this point. The Pip barely stammered out, "Who mooed?"

"Why, Sally did. Damnedest thing I ever heard. She sounded like a prime heifer early on a spring morning. Don't know any other way to say it. She mooed like a damn cow. And kept mooing. I remember wondering if I could get her to stop, 'cause I knew Terry and Lassie had to hear it, but I stopped worryin' about that quick. What would you do? Worry about them, or the matter at hand? That's a decision even Bobby Cox could make!

"I got serious again, and we proceeded to roll like tractors, mooing be damned. Things were going really well until I heard a knock at the door.

"I heard that damn Terry say, 'Are y'all all right in there?'

"I like Terry a lot, but I thought it was the stupidest question I had ever been asked. Sally answered him, hollering out, 'What in the hell do you think, Terry? Go get my purse from the kitchen, pull out a twenty, and y'all take your asses to a damn movie!'

"Ol' Terry shut the hell up, and I respected Sally even

more. Look, I was about to make like Cape Canaveral and blast-off the Williams' rocket, so I wasn't gonna waste any more time thinkin' of Terry and the haint princess. It was time to take care of some extremely urgent groinocological business."

At this point, we weren't even urging Ed Jr. to take it easy anymore. We knew that it was our destiny to hear him out, so we held our aching stomachs and continued listening. Ray even urged him on, saying, "Tell it, Godfather."

"I did what I had to do, and when I did, Sally mooed like the head production cow at a milkshake factory. She hollered, called out my name, belted out a couple of U.S. presidents' names, and said God knows what else. I really couldn't pick it all up, as I was pretty much out of it, but she was singing like a bed of crickets."

Ray looked up at this point, winked over at Hugh and me, and said, "Godfather, why do you think we want to hear about two old farts like y'all knocking it out? It's getting me to the point where I don't even want to eat these wings anymore."

Ed Jr. shot back, "I'll stop tellin' you young bucks about this if y'all can tell me something you did recently that was better."

He had us all to rights there. Hugh said that he had no recent experiences in this vein that he could discuss. Ray laughed and said if he got a hot meal a couple of nights a week, his life was exciting. Personally, I just sat there and told Ed Jr. that none of us could hold a candle to the Godfather, and we all admitted it. Satisfied that he had made his point, he went on.

"I thought as much. Smartass young bucks!"

After a pause for effect, he continued. "Sally and I had a helluva time, no doubt about it, and we both ended up feeling real good.

"After a while, I walked into her kitchen and checked the time. She was right along beside me, although the robe she now had on wouldn't have covered a gnat's ass. Then, noting that Terry and the Alpo commercial were gone, I said my goodbyes to Sally, and I went home and slept like a dead man."

Ed Jr. turned mute at that point. For a moment, he got a pensive expression on his face. The curiosity was about to kill me, so I had to pose the question: "Dad, what happened between you and Sally after that? Do y'all still see each other?"

"Well, boy, to tell you the truth, I liked ol' Sally a lot, but it just wasn't meant to be. She did call me several times after that, wanting to saddle up the Ed Williams bronco, but I just couldn't see her anymore. Nice as she was, I just couldn't."

"Why?"

"Would you want to get sweet on a woman who reminds you of a record full of barnyard noises? Would you? Hell, when I was driving home from her house, all I could think of was cows and horses and stuff. Not the kind of thinkin' I want to do after I've downloaded my trousers' personal files."

We all congratulated Ed Jr. on using current phrases to capture the essence of tulip honing. He laughed right along with us, then paused for a second, and added, "Just remember this much, and I'll tell y'all this 'til the day I die, 'cause it's important. No one ever did anything by sitting back—you have to be a man of action. Me, I live for action. I make stuff happen. I know I'm Ed Williams Jr., and that I have one time to do whatever it is that I want to do. And I do it. And among those things most important to me is the ability to enjoy the company of a good woman. What's better than that? Let's face it—the day that I can't be with a woman, or eat, I hope that one of y'all will have the gumption to put my poor ass out of its misery. Life is too short not to live it to the fullest, and no one is fuller of life than me!"

We just paused and stared at him. At that moment, I guess Ray, Hugh, and I realized that we'd just been given, in a few sentences, the total essence of Ed Jr. A man who loved his women and food. A man who had his priorities worked out. A man who was focused and knew what he was, and why he was put here on this earth. Ultimately, a man who had imparted a tender love story to the Brotherhood.

Southern Fried Farce Contributors

Roy Blount Jr.:

Roy Blount Jr. is the author of twenty books, including *Crackers*; *Roy Blount's Book of Southern Humor*; *Feet on the Street: Rambles About New Orleans*; and *Long Time Leaving: Dispatches From Up South*. His work has appeared in *The New Yorker, The New York Times*, the *Atlantic Monthly*, *Sports Illustrated* and many other publications. He is a columnist for *The Oxford American* and a panelist on NPR's "Wait, Wait...Don't Tell Me."

Lisa Daily:

Lisa Daily is the bestselling author of a dating advice book called *Stop Getting Dumped!* and a novel entitled *Fifteen Minutes of Shame*. Lisa lives in Florida. (South Florida, of course.) For more on Lisa, visit www.stopgettingdumped.com.

M.L. Davis:

M.L. Davis is the pen name of Maria D. Baisier, who lives in New Orleans. She has written a book *Pieces: Putting Life Back Together After Loss* (Davis, Xlibris), and three of her essays under the name Baisier appear in the book *Katrina: Mississippi Women Remember* (University Press). Her short story "Never Too Late" appeared in *Woman's World Magazine*, and her essay "Changing Demographics" received an award at the Eugene Walters Writers' Festival at the University of South Alabama. She is a teacher and theatre director.

Jim Dees:

Jim Dees writes a weekly newspaper column, "Lies and Other Truths," and is the host of Thacker Mountain Radio, a music and literature program on Mississippi Public Broadcasting. He is the editor of *They Write Among Us,* an anthology of Southern writing. Dees lives in Taylor, Mississippi.

John T. Edge:

John T. Edge is director of the Southern Foodways Alliance at the University of Mississippi in Oxford. He is a contributing writer for *The Oxford American*, a contributing editor for *Gourmet*, and a columnist for the *Atlanta Journal-Constitution*, among others. He wrote and reported "I'm Not Leaving Until I Eat This Thing" in the days leading up to his marriage.

CLYDE EDGERTON:

Clyde Edgerton is the author of eight novels and a work of non-fiction. He teaches in the MFA program at UNC-Wilmington. His life is unassuming and gentle, full of long beach walks and solitude. He shuns publicity. A glossy, autographed 8 x 10 of him in beard and hunting shirt is available through Edgerton Productions, 492 Amber Ave, Wilmington, NC, 28403. A two-for-one special will be on through September of 2009.

TOM FRANKLIN:

Tom Franklin has published a collection of stories, *Poachers*, whose title novella won the Edgar Allan Poe Award. His novel *Hell at the Breech* won the Mississippi Institute of Arts and Letters prize and the Alabama Library Award for Adult Fiction. His most recent novel is *Smonk*, a finalist for the Southern Independent Booksellers award. Winner of a 2001 Guggenheim Fellowship, he is a writer-in-residence at the University of Mississippi and lives in Oxford with his wife, poet Beth Ann Fennelly, and their two children.

WILLIAM GAY:

William Gay is the author of three novels and a collection of stories and various pieces about music for *The Oxford American* and *Paste*. His short fiction has appeared in several anthologies, including *Best of the South*, *The O. Henry Prize Stories*, and *Best American Short Stories*. He lives in Hohenwald, Tennessee.

David Magee:

David Magee is the author of eight non-fiction books, including *The South is Round* and *MoonPie*. Compared by *Kirkus Reviews* to the late Lewis Grizzard and by *Booklist* to Dave Barry, Magee's subjects include southern culture, business, and sports. His book *Turnaround*, called a "provocative case study" by *Harvard Business Review*, has sold more than 100,000 copies worldwide, while his most recent book, *How Toyota Became #1*, is an inside study of the world's largest automaker. A co-owner of Chattanooga's Rock Point Books, Magee lives on Lookout Mountain, Tennessee, with his wife and three children.

Lisa Earle McLeod:

A top-selling author, nationally syndicated columnist, and media personality, Lisa is an expert in corporate disillusionment, mommy guilt, slacker parenting, faux housework, managerial misery, flat-line libidos, and drive-thru spirituality. She has appeared on *Good Morning America*, *ABC News*, and *Oprah & Friends*. Her work has been featured in *The Wall Street Journal*, *The New York Times*, *USA Today*, *Newsweek*, *Essence*, and *O Magazine*.

Lewis Nordan:

Lewis Nordan is the author of four story collections, three novels, including *The Sharpshooter Blues*, which won the American Library Association's Notable Book Award, and the memoir, *Boy With Loaded Gun*. He is the recipient of a best fiction award from the Mississippi Institute of Arts and Letters, and is now retired from his teaching position at the University of Pittsburgh, where he instructed creative writing.

Jack Pendarvis:

Jack Pendarvis is the author of two story collections, *The Mysterious Secret of the Valuable Treasure* and *Your Body Is Changing*. His work has appeared in *McSweeny's*, *The Believer*, and *The Oxford American*, and his stories have been anthologized in the Pushcart Prize anthology and elsewhere. He currently serves as the John and Renee Grisham Writer-in-Residence at the University of Mississippi.

Susan Reinhardt:

Susan Reinhardt is the award-winning author of *Not Tonight Honey, Wait 'til I'm a Size 6* and *Don't Sleep with a Bubba*. A syndicated columnist for Gannett newspapers, her features have appeared in the *Washington Post*, *London Daily Mirror*, and *Newsday*. Reinhardt was born in South Carolina, raised in Georgia, and currently lives in Asheville, North Carolina.

Celia Rivenbark:

Celia Rivenbark is an award-winning newspaper columnist and author of national bestsellers *Bless Your Heart, Tramp* and *We're Just Like You, Only Prettier*. Her third book, *Stop Dressing Your Six Year Old Like A Skank*, was named Best Title of 2006 by *Entertainment Weekly* magazine. A syndicated humor columnist,

Celia's work has appeared in *Southern Living, USA Today, Reader's Digest,* and *The New York Times.* She lives in Wilmington, North Carolina, with her husband and daughter.

GEORGE SINGLETON:

George Singleton has published the collections *These People Are Us, The Half-Mammals of Dixie, Why Dogs Chase Cars,* and *Drowning in Gruel.* His novels are *Novel* and *Work Shirts for Madmen.* Singleton's short stories have appeared in *The Atlantic Monthly, Harper's, Playboy, Zoetrope, The Georgia Review, Shenandoah,* and elsewhere. He lives in Dacusville, South Carolina, and teaches at the S.C. Governor's School for the Arts.

JAMES WHORTON JR.

James Whorton Jr. is a prizewinning short story writer and author of two novels, *Approximately Heaven* and *Frankland.* He was raised in Florida and Mississippi and now lives in Rochester, New York, with his wife and their daughter.

ED WILLIAMS:

Ed Williams is a true genetic Southerner who hails from Juliette, Georgia. He's the author of the books *Sex, Dead Dogs, and Me: The Juliette Journals,* and *Rough As A Cob: More From the Juliette Journals.* He also loves ICEEs, Bachman-Turner Overdrive, Atomic Fireballs, and anyone who appreciates honin' a good tulip.